Early Praise

"Broken Pencils is a singular feat of narrative momentum. Dauntless insight and camera angle dance sharply producing a new geometry of storytelling."

— Tongo Eisen-Martin, Poet laureate of San Francisco, California, activist, and author

"Rice offers an emotionally resonant, thoughtful, and philosophically charged narrative in Broken Pencils. It serves as a compelling reminder of the weight of our choices and their indelible impact on our lives and those around us."

— Karen Almeida, *Literary Titan*

"Broken Pencils pulls you down a complex river of identity, coming-of-age, mental illness, and issues of class and race in a way that taps into the universal experience of being human, all while couched in the skilled prose of a literary masterpiece."

—M.M. Chouinard, USA Today bestselling author of *The Dancing Girls*

"J.R. Rice drives the reader headlong through the looking glass of Jonah Tarver's soul — and oh what ride. It is both hypnotic and often hallucinatory, but ultimately a journey of devastating truth."

— Andrew L. Roberts, Author of *Tears for Shulna*

"Rice weaves together moments of heartache, triumph, and introspection with such vividness that it feels like peering into real lives rather than fictional characters. This authenticity deepens the emotional impact felt by the reader and truly makes this book a must read."

— *Literary Global*

"Compelling and vulnerable, Broken Pencils is a poetic peek inside what it means to feel surrounded and alone at the same time. It juxtaposes the safety and simplicity of childhood against the illusion of freedom that adulthood brings."

— Angela Drew, Author of *ElderBerry Wine*

"The book underscores the vital importance of seeking help to heal mentally and find inner peace, as carrying pain for too long can impede progress."

— Amanda Hanson, *The US Review of Books*

"In this visceral odyssey through a single night, the reader is enveloped in Jonah's gut-wrenching journey toward clarity and acceptance...If there ever was a flawed hero to root for, it's Rice's modern-day Odysseus, Jonah."

— Rosa del Duca, Author of *Breaking Cadence*

"The action of the book is full-throttle, but the story is also gripping because of Rice's multi-layered storytelling. It's rare that a book achieves this intensity of suspense and is also philosophically and psychologically resonant."

— Heidi Kasa, Award-Winning author of *The Beginners*

"The raw and introspective prose invites empathy and reflection, while also captivating readers with vivid imagery, poignant reflections, and authentic dialogue."

— Neena H. Brar, *The Prairies Book Reviews*

"Author JR Rice has indeed illuminated a subject matter that deserves to be revisited. Starting with an important question, What can we do as a village to raise and protect the Jonah's of the world?"

— Monique McCoy, Author of *Poetry's Daughter*

"J.R Rice deftly uses Langston Hughes' work as both a structural and spiritual template...Rice emerges with his own voice as a life affirming force and a literary badass!"

— Dr. Mtafiti Imara, Professor of Music at Cal State University, San Marcos, and jazz composer

"Filled with youthful exuberance, raucous partying, vicious truths, and heartbreaking volatility, Broken Pencils is a novel that aims for poignancy, targeting an age group where many struggle to find meaning."

— R.C. Gibson, *IndiesToday*

"As he tries to make sense of his life, Jonah rides through Rice's use of metaphors, poem excerpts, song lyrics, and the never ending quote, 'Still no cure for the common birthday.' Rice's use of imagination makes for a fantastical tale of what it means to be alive."

— Leticia Garcia Bradford, editor and publisher at *MoonShine Star Co*

"Broken Pencils tackles a sensitive and difficult topic in a meaningful way that provides food for thought and allows one to become introspective about mental illness and the difficulties faced by those who live with it."

— Jennie More, *Readers' Favorite*

"Rice's writing pulls you into the edgy emotions of a young man caught between a strict and successful father, freewheeling friends, and his inability to shed past sorrow and make sense of his future. Broken Pencils catapults you into the complex emotional rhythms of a teen on the cusp of adulthood."

— Tish Davidson, Author of *From War Room to Living Room*

"Broken Pencils is an in-your-face category five hurricane of written words. A beautifully written, yet tragic and gritty reminder that we are the choices we make."

— Tony Aldarondo, Author of *Poet on the Run*

"Broken Pencils tackles youth and mental illness with an authenticity and sincerity that lingers with you long after you've finished reading."

— Jason Baum, Author of *Rocket*

BROKEN PENCILS

PENCILS

J.R. RICE

To my father, Dion, and Trevon.

Contents

Teacher
by Langston Hughes

Ideals are like the stars,
Always above our reach.
Humbly I tried to learn,
More humbly did I teach.
On all honest virtues
I sought to keep firm hold.
I wanted to be a good man
Though I pinched my soul.
But now I lie beneath cool loam
Forgetting every dream;
And in this narrow bed of earth
No lights gleam.
In this narrow bed of earth
Star-dust never scatters,
And I tremble lest the darkness teach
Me that nothing matters.

PROLOGUE
MOSSWOOD

S irens jolted my senses. Blue and red lights blinded my sight. Within my blurry vision appeared a parked police car. Loud static erupted from inside. And then it hit me.

My bed was a bench.

"No loiterers in Mosswood park before six a.m," a male voice said. *"Please vacate."*

The warm sunrise caressed my cold face and stiff body. My bandaged hand wiped the dry crust from my eyes then smeared the grime onto the bench. The Kaiser hospital stood across the street, the place where I was born eighteen years ago today. Behind the bench stood a yellow sign that stated: *Looking for a better home?* Under the banner was an Asian lady with this constipated Mona Lisa smile. She wore an eighties tan suit straight from Claire Huxable's closet, an outfit my mama would have worn back in the day, when life was simple, our family happy. Before Keon. Before the medication. Before prom.

"Please vacate the park now," the voice ordered.

The ringing sirens screamed louder and louder, deafening my ears. The looped circus whistle rang far and wide, awaking all of Mosswood Park. Within moments, dawn broke through the tall oak trees. The bushy leaves casted a shadow through which no light traveled. Then the ground rumbled as the bench rattled. Three brown squirrels sprinted across the grassy field. A roaring street sweeper had arrived at the corner of the MacArthur sign. The machine's brush-like tentacles rustled and roamed along the curb lines, moving slowly around a parked beige Mercedes. The scraped front bumper appeared to have survived a bear attack.

"Is that my father's car?" I whispered into the cool air, already knowing the answer.

The sirens ceased singing. The police car lights stopped flashing. Within the stillness stirred sharp aches in my unsettled stomach. Each deep breath felt like an alien embryo begging to burst from my belly. The longer I laid on that dead bench, the more I felt like dying. My safe space was no longer a safe place. I had to leave. I needed to go, but where?

The police car door opened. A Black officer stepped out wearing a navy-blue uniform. His broad shoulders and toned biceps barely fit into his short-sleeve shirt. He walked around the car, stopped in front of the bench, and studied my appearance. His right hand hung centimeters from his sidearm.

"What are you doing here?" the officer asked. "Were you sleeping on the bench?"

"I don't know," I lied.

I shook my head and rolled my body over to the bench's edge. Laying on my stomach eased the pain a bit. My arms hung lifeless. My fingers traced the sidewalk cracks and concrete veins. The lines led in no apparent direction as if I was staring at my own reflection. Then the ground began spiraling, spinning my eyes. My body retreated, curling into a fetal position.

"Sit up," the officer ordered. "I need you to talk."

He lowered himself to my eye level. His brown eyes appeared as dark and bold as his complexion. His chiseled face, trimmed goatee, and no-shit attitude reminded me of Denzel Washington's character in *Training Day*, Keon's favorite movie.

"What happened to your hands?" he asked and pointed to my bandages with dried blood.

"I don't even know anymore."

"Let's start here," he said and tapped his O.P.D badge. "My name is Officer Williams. What's your name?"

3

"Name?"

"Don't tell me you don't know who you are."

I shook my head again and sat up straight, cringing with each stretch.

"My name? My *real* name is Jonah Tarver."

"Okay Jonah, got any I.D?" Officer Williams asked.

I noticed him noticing the remains of my tuxedo: An unbuttoned white shirt, loosen bow tie, smeared make-up on my shoulder, and black slacks covered in a brown-yellow shit color. I patted my pockets, not once, not twice. Ten times. This present reality and past recollection had both smacked me at the same damn time. My money, phone, car keys were stolen by that lying-ass bitch. The strangest part was that I couldn't recall when or how everything went wrong.

"I don't know what I'm doing. I don't know where I'm going or who I am."

"Were you at a prom?" he asked and looked around the park. "Is this some kind of joke?"

"Yeah, life is just a big joke, and guess what? God is the comedian."

"Funny. Now tell me the truth, what's going on? Have you taken any drugs or alcohol?"

"I don't know. All I know, all I know is *'In this narrow bed of earth, no lights gleam, in this narrow bed of earth'* ahh shit." My lips tried to recite the Langston Hughes poem, but my mind forgot the lines again. At this point, the words served no purpose. "No, I still can't remember why. Why do I need to remember?"

"What's the problem, Jonah?" he asked.

"Who said I had a problem? I don't have a problem. What's your problem?"

My head rattled, unable to make sense of the situation. Resolve: Leave, go, run, but where? My body summoned whatever energy left stored and rose from the bench like a vampire out of a coffin. My feet felt sore and heavy on the sidewalk as if I had been walking all night. I attempted to march the other direction. My small steps wobbled like a toddler. I moved past Officer Williams' right side, gaining a few feet from the bench. He followed me.

"I wish, I wish, I wish you'd go away."

"Where are you going?" he hollered. "We're not done."

I passed Officer Williams by several meters. My pace increased with each step, making it difficult for him to keep up. Then he ran after me, so my legs ran even faster. My mind paid no attention to my runny nose, pounding heart, and panting lungs. My four-years track intuition had already kicked in, yet the finish line was beyond my sight, only a looming breakdown.

"Stop, dammit," he shouted at my back.

My feet reached the end of the block. As I caught my breath, he grabbed hold of my arm.

"Let go," I shouted and tried to shake off his grip. "I said, let me go!"

"Control yourself, son," he said and squeezed my arm tighter. He reached for the radio strapped to his shoulder.

"No, let me go. Don't you see? I want to die. I fucking mean it."

My soul began to burst. A scream erupted from my lungs, disrupting the morning stillness. The sound of fury forced Officer Williams to release my arm and take a step back.

"Jonah, relax, be still," he said. His mouth gasped. His eyes shifted back and forth. His torso turned rigid. "Please, son."

My fingers started to tingle, tremble, and then transform into fists.

"No, I'm not your son. Don't call me that. I'm not you're fucking son, so just stop it. I don't give a fuck anymore, so just do it already, shoot, just shoot. Come on, put me out of my misery. I know you want to."

"What are you saying?" He stepped closer. "You don't want to die. Let me help you."

Dr. Imani had said those words long ago. So did my mama, father, and Taniesha. Now I was given the offer by a complete stranger.

"Jonah, let me help you," Officer Williams repeated and opened his hand.

"Fuck you."

"What'd you just say?" he asked and dropped his hand to his sidearm.

My body was shaking. A shiver ran down my spine. My body grew comfortably
numb as weightless words slipped from my tongue.

"You heard me cop. Come on, you fucking pig. You think you know me, but you don't know my life and the pointless shit I've been through. You don't know that I feel so sick and tired of being sick and tired. I just want it to stop. I can't live like this. I need help."

I fell to my knees. My shoulders collapsed forward. My legs nearly toppled onto the ground. My arms unfolded onto the concrete. My hands begged the sky.

"I'm not okay. I'm not alright."

"You will be okay," he said. "You will be alright."

Officer Williams extended his hand. Without hesitation, I grabbed the invitation. He didn't have warrior palms nor did his stature resemble a knight. His hands had the gentleness of real strength. He reminded me of an older, more mature Keon, if he had lived to see his thirties. My best friend would have gone into law enforcement after high school, if he had lived to see his graduation. Everything would've been different, if Keon had survived the car accident.

"Help me," I pleaded.

"It's okay," Officer Williams said. "Trust me, life is simple. We just make it complex."

He lifted me up to my feet, turned to his side, and searched his black utility belt.

"For your own safety, I'm going to put you in cuffs. You're not under arrest. I don't want you hurting yourself or someone else. You understand?"

I nodded knowingly.

"Can you turn around? These cuffs might feel a little tight."

I straightened my arms behind my back. He stood over my shadow and patted my pants. His hands reached inside each pocket then pulled out the neon bracelet, my only innocence.

"Who is, wait, does that say *Taniesha*? You know what? I'll let you hold onto this one."

Officer Williams placed the bracelet back into my pocket. We walked side by side back to the police car. He opened the door and placed his hand on my head. I slipped into the back seat. He started the car and pressed several keys on the dashboard computer.

"Your info should come up in a second," he said. "How are you doing back there?"

"Fine, I'm fine," I lied with squinted eyes, fighting a well of tears.

"Let's see, Jonah, Jonah Tarver, ah, here we go. You live on 323 Parkcrest Street by Skyline? It says today is your eighteenth birthday." He laughed. "There's still no cure for the common birthday, you know."

"Thanks. I almost forgot."

"I see that Mercedes parked there is registered to your pops. Wait, wait, are you the son of Superior Court Judge Tarver? This'll be interesting."

I nodded and stared out the tinted window. A brown squirrel climbed onto the bench, standing on his two hind legs. His black nose sniffed the air. His dark eyes set on a faded sunrise. Perhaps in another life, we had switched places without remorse.

"Hold on, wait a second," Officer Williams said. His face grew anxious as he continued studying the glowing LCD screen. "Says here that you were involved in an assault and battery last night in San Francisco, less than six hours ago."

My head leaned against the black cage barrier. "I want to go home."

He picked up his radio. "I don't think so."

CHAPTER 1
HOME

F riday 6:02 p.m.

"They're arguing again," Steven said and pointed to the sounds outside his bedroom. "But like really, *really* loud this time."

"I know, but don't worry," I said and closed the door. "It's never about you."

My father's voice reverberated into Steven's room, even from downstairs. My seven-year old brother jumped off his bed and dropped his action figures onto the Captain America rug. He pulled up his saggy Spongebob pajamas and then tugged on my black slacks. His brown skin was lighter than mine, unblemished by regret.

"Wait, wait, what's a...a *ali-mooney*?" he asked. His teary eyes looked up at mine.

"Why do you want to know about alimony?" I replied and pulled the Nordstrom bag from around my back.

"Ahlee-mo-knee," he pronounced slowly. "That's what mama said to daddy."

"Don't worry, okay. Just ignore all that stuff like I told you."

I set the bag near his side. He didn't notice or care.

"But, but I don't like it when, when they yell," he stuttered like usual when upset. His small lips trembled. His button nose was runny, sniffling with each word. "Why mama and daddy not happy?"

"Never blame yourself. I stopped a long time ago."

I pulled out a folded tissue and sat down across from my little brother. My legs twisted into a Buddha-like style to mimic his position. I handed Steven the tissue and then patted his wrinkled yellow Curious George shirt, so he'd look neat for mama. He blew his nose as loud as an elephant, but his body continued to fidget. When I held his soft hand, he found his calm.

"Bless you," I said and gave a fake laugh. "Sounded like your soul left your body."

"What that mean?" Steven asked and slid his hand away from mine.

"I hope you never know." I handed him the bag. "So anyways, are you going to do that thing for me after I leave?"

"I said yeah, sheesh," he replied and juggled the bag. He noticed the two orange medicine bottles. "Why, why hide your pills? Don't you need them? When you come back from prom? Can't you stay and play with me?"

"I told you, mama checks everything I do, except with you. And no, I can't play right now, but I'll be home when you wake up, promise."

"I don't believe you," he said and shook his head. "You don't act like Jonah no more."

"Why do you say that?"

"I don't know. You don't play with me no more. I don't, I don't want to talk."

Steven slouched forward with the weight of frustration burdening his short posture.

"How about an early 'Happy birthday' shout-out or something?" I asked, but his head was turned away. "I'm still your big Bro-Namath, Bro-Schmo, Bro-Montana, you're come on, bro, do you remember?"

His head turned, but a frown face had emerged to sing, *"Happy, happy birthday Bro-tato!* Happy? Goodbye now."

"Thanks little bruh, and never say goodbye. Always, see you later."

"Whatever," he said and reached for his action figures.

"Humbly I tried to learn, more humbly did I teach."

A grin glimmered from his parted mouth. His brown face glowed before my eyes then the light quickly disappeared. Steven turned his back to me and reverted to his former activity. My little brother became a passionate puppeteer with his toys. He moved the figures around the rug, recreating a vast world of his own. His voice deepened, imitating the foreign speech of the characters. Roars, growls, and slicing sounds escaped from his mouth. Much like myself, my little brother was lost in his own fantasy.

Steven didn't look up as I walked out the door.

Curious about the commotion, I peeked my head toward the staircase. As expected, my mama and father stood downstairs in a stance fitting of two opposing gladiators, except they were in suburban attire. My father wore a brown polo shirt, khaki slacks, and suede loafers, his idea of casual dress. My mama wore a blue blouse and a long satin skirt as if she expected company to arrive. They both occupied the living room space, standing with their arms crossed and their legs parted like they were about to play a W.W.E style round of rock, paper, scissors.

Everything in the living room was perfectly set the same as it was an hour ago when I left to get dressed. The mud-colored modular sofa sat in the corner next to the villainous Strandmon chair. The IKEA virus had spread into my home as soon as my mama began to collect the catalogs. She treated each one like a priceless magazine. Once the furniture porn infected her mind, the IKEA virus then spread into my father's head. This was at the same time he accepted the Superior Court judge job and Steven was born. Within seven odd years, our family went from well-off Black folks to superficial Swedes.

"All those therapy appointments, evals, and extra counseling outside of Kaiser had cost almost a thousand dollars last month," my father said. "Out of pocket, *my* pocket."

His stern voice had carried all the way upstairs. My body hid behind the railing and kept cover from his six-foot-five bulky frame facing my direction. At any moment, my father could have looked up and noticed my eavesdropping.

"It's always about money with you," my mama said. "I don't see why that matters now."

"It's not about the money, so don't go there," he said. "How long has he been seeing Dr. Imani? It's been about four years now, Janine. What's changed since he was caught shoplifting only a month ago? Now we're getting calls saying he's truant again, skipping out on sessions again, and pulling these tantrums everywhere like a little boy *again*."

"Our young man is getting dressed," she said and pointed upstairs. I lowered my head, peeking through the railing. "You want to tell him he can't go?"

"Don't make me the bad guy," he said and raised his finger to her face. "Do you know for sure he's even taking his prescriptions?"

"I check. Do you think I don't know my own son? Maybe if you spent more time."

"We've had this discussion already. The boy doesn't talk to me."

"Please, can we talk about this later after he leaves?"

"When do you suppose we'll tell him the other news? He probably knows already."

"I don't know, Terry. Both of them might not be ready. And honestly, neither am I."

Their voices grew low and hard to hear, so I leaned closer against the bar railing.

"I want tonight to be good for Jonah," she said. "I want him to feel like a normal teenager for once. Okay, that's it. I'm going to check again to see if he's done."

"No, you went up already," he said. "I'll check."

A silence stomped into the living room. My parents exchanged nods then walked in separate directions. My mama went to the shelf, picked up her camera, and then placed it on the coffee table. My father went to the staircase. He saw me at the top stair, crouching on the floor. I stood up, patted the sleeves of my tuxedo jacket, and waved my wrists like jazz hands.

"How do I look?" I asked.

"Proud," my father said and examined my attire. He nodded with approval. "The tux fits you better than the one from my wedding. How long have you been sitting there?"

"Not long. What were you two talking about?"

"You...always," he mumbled.

My mama walked over and stood next to my father.

"Jonah," she said, glowing with excitement. "You're looking very handsome with your little bow tie like a

Black James Bond. Here we thought Mr. GQ was still getting dressed."

"Thanks mama. Hey, can I borrow your car? I want to pick up Taniesha and Trevon, and then head to Frisco. I forgot to tell you the prom is at the Old Federal Reserve building."

"Oh, that's no biggie. I thought you were taking a limo with your other friends."

"I changed my mind."

My parents glanced at each other at the same time, exchanging some kind of secret signal. I could only assume the worst.

"So, how's Taniesha doing by the way?" she asked. "You need to bring her over for dinner again so she can finally meet your father. But that's for another time. Hurry down. We need to take a few pictures before you go. First, I got you a little something for your birthday."

My mama stepped out of the living room into the kitchen. I walked down the stairs and met my father with a forced smile. He rubbed my shoulder, dug his fingers into my muscles, and then dog-patted my head. I nodded and continued to smile until he retreated to the couch. My mama returned from the kitchen, skipping into the room. Her arms hid behind her back. My father grunted and grabbed his wine glass off the coffee table.

"Here you go," she said. "Enjoy."

I watched her arms move around to her waist and handed me a wrapped rectangular gift.

"I know it's still early and all, but I wanted your night to start off well. There's still no cure for the common birthday."

"What's that supposed to mean?" I asked and knocked on the gift. "Feels like a book."

"Open it and see."

I ripped open the wrapping. "It's a...a journal?"

"Don't look too excited, yeah, there's some money in there too." She frowned and pointed to the black leather binding. "It's like the one Dr. Imani gave to you a while back. I saw the other one you had was filled up, so I went ahead and got you another."

"Have you been going through his personal stuff, Janine?" my father asked and rose from his seat. My mama took a step back. "You didn't read his journal, did you?"

"Relax. I glanced at it, that's all," she admitted.

"Mama?"

"I'm happy you're getting your thoughts out like she suggested. I feel so pleased seeing you write. I always see you reading something like that book of quotes you carry around. I hope you know that you make me, I mean, you make us so proud, especially going to college, but I do worry about you sometimes."

"Fine, I'm fine," I lied and removed two $100 dollar bills tucked inside the cover. I threw the journal on the coffee table. "Just fine and dandy like cotton candy."

She reached for a hug. Her cheek pressed to my ear.

"You say 'I'm fine' all the time," she whispered. "Then I see you moping around most of the week like something's troubling you. What's wrong sweetheart?"

"Janine," he said and stomped his foot. "Let it go."

"It's okay," I said and released myself from her hug.

"Now listen boy, don't act too surprised by my gift, especially now that you need it," my father said and pulled out a remote car key from his pocket. "But since you're turning eighteen and your prom is tonight, I've decided to lend you the Mercedes. I want you and your date, Tiesha, I mean, Taniesha to go in style, but don't you act uncivilized with my property. Listen, I know what that boy Trevon gets into. I don't approve, but I'm not going to pry. With my car comes no drinking or drugs, no speeding or playing taxi for some hooligans. Don't do anything that will dishonor the family. You hear me?"

"No fun," I uttered under my breath.

"What'd you say?" he asked and shrugged my arm. "You listening?"

"Yes, I'm listening. I understand. Thank you."

"Thank you what?"

"Thank you, sir."

Sunset glimmered through the closed curtains. Silence filled the room again. Steven shouted from upstairs. My father nodded with satisfaction and dropped the key into my palm. He sat back on the couch and sipped his wine. My mama rolled her eyes and forced a smile.

"Picture time," she said and picked up her camera. "Hold still. I want a good one to give to granny and your girlfriend."

I tugged on my jacket sleeve. My cuffs were caught on the neon bracelet.

"Hold it, hold still, and stop messing with that little thing," she insisted.

"Wait, Taniesha would kill me if I didn't show off my bracelet. Okay, am I good now?"

She moved to the left and right, snapping several more pictures from different angles.

"Now I want one with the both of you," she said and elbowed my father. "Then we can try to do one with the whole family. Terry, stand next to your son."

My father and I stood together, only connected by our shoulders.

"Straighten up," he ordered. "Don't slouch."

The light illuminated from the camera.

"I'm not slouching. You are." I turned away from him. "Mama, turn off the flash."

"Okay, but wait, let me get your brother," she said and stepped toward the staircase. "Steven! Come down for a second, dear. Steven! What's that boy doing up there?"

"Stop being difficult," he said.

"I'm not being difficult. You are."

"Do this for your mother," he replied.

"What did you just say?"

"You heard me, boy. Do this for your mother," he repeated slowly.

Perhaps my father didn't remember or wasn't aware of his exact words. He had said the same line when he wanted me to go to Keon's funeral, in spite of my refusal.

"Why does it matter anyway? You don't care."

"Really? Funny thing is you don't even realize how good you have it," he said.

"Terry, don't start this right now, please," she pleaded.

"No, the boy needs to hear this," he told her and stepped out of the picture frame. He pointed to various parts in the room. "Your mother and I give every necessity for you and your brother. You have a home, phone, clothes, sheesh, we let you borrow the car. Don't you know your great-grandfather became a freed slave at eighteen? When I was your age, I didn't have the luxuries you call your own, neither did your mother. We were the first ones in our family's history to graduate college, yet here you are, acting like this, like you're spoiled rotten."

My mama moved in closer and rubbed my father's shoulders.

"Okay no more photos," she said. "Let's all take a time-out."

"It's fine, I was already done," I said. "None of this matters since he ain't here."

"Then what matters, son?" he asked, shaking his head.

"Terry," she interrupted. "This ain't the right time."

"What matters is that I love you," he continued, ignoring my mama. "I love this family, and I'll do whatever possible to make sure all of you are alright.

But son, there's something you must do. Let go of what's eating you up inside. You can't blame us for what happened. Like Dr. Imani said, there's no need to hide it. I love you. I'm sorry, but Keon is gone."

"Why did you say that?" My eyes snapped shut. "No, don't say that."

I love you, I'm sorry, I love you, I'm sorry, Keon is...

Darkness covered my eyes. My mind replayed each word my father had said, seeing my thirteen year-old self in the same place, but a different time. The morning before my birthday. Alone downstairs. Living room couch. *Ring. Ring. Ring.* Upstairs landline. *Click.* My ears eavesdropped on my father and Keon's mom. Then the worst news I'd ever hear in my life. Dropped phone. House door slammed. Legs running toward an escape. Running until out of breath. Pausing. Then running again. Finding a park with no name. Sitting on the bench, tired in tears, asking the sky: *Why did my best friend have to die?* Hours, minutes, seconds passed in loneliness. My father arrived to find a life broken. He carried my pieces into the car. "I love you, I'm sorry, but Keon is gone." I had already known after overhearing the news on the phone. "It was no one's fault." Back home. Kitchen. "Drink this to calm down." Boiling pot. Warm tea. "Come upstairs when you're ready." His full embrace followed by his feet in retreat. Grief and I fled to the bathroom. Door locked. Broken razor. Slit left wrist in shock. Darkness.

My eyes opened wide.

"Did you hear me? Where did you go?" my father asked.

"It's fucking bullshit," I said.

My father's face lit up in shock.

"Sorry, say that again," he said. "I don't think I heard you."

"I'm sick and tired of this bullshit," I said louder.

"Don't you use that language with me. You're still a boy. I don't care how old you are."

My mama stepped in between us.

"Stop it, both of you," she ordered. "Calm down, Terry."

"I'm not the one acting like I don't have sense. He's having one of his episodes *again*."

I straightened up and faced him.

"Fuck you. Fuck you."

My father slapped my face. His sweaty palms pierced my cheek, nearly snapping my neck. The sting riddled my body, rocking my feet. My eyes went blurry, unsteady. My ears deafened by the wind. Minutes in the dark turned into seconds outside of consciousness. When the light appeared again, my father was wiping his hands with a small towel.

"Don't you ever speak to me like that," he said.

My mama's fingers caressed my bruised face. I stood up and brushed away her affection.

"Wait a minute, son," she said.

I waved my farewell.

"Sorry mama, I tried like we promised, but I can't do this no more."

"Boy, sit down," my father ordered and pointed his finger at the empty chair.

"No," I replied.

"Where's the key, boy?"

"No."

"Boy, give me the key."

My father reached for my pocket. I backed away and clenched the key. He squeezed my arm, pulling me near. I elbowed his ribs. His grip released. We stepped apart. My mama held onto his side. They hugged and weeped, unable to see beyond their disappointment.

"No more. I'm nobody's boy."

I walked away from my parents who felt like strangers. My lifeless legs floated through the living room and toward a dark garage. My trembling body stopped at the door, resisting the urge to turn around. Seconds passed in silence. No one followed because no one was coming.

I twisted the handle and held the door open. My eyes stared at the beige Mercedes in the darkness and marched inside without looking back. As soon as I reached the car, the garage light turned on.

"See you later," a voice whispered.

CHAPTER 2
TEACHER

F riday 7:07 p.m.

"Not all pussy is the same, every pussy is different," Trevon said. My best friend of three years parted his thick dreadlocks from his brown face. He poked his nose out the passenger side window and sniffed the cool evening breeze. "Listen up bruh, I'm going to teach you some shit."

Trevon and I descended down the Oakland hills, driving past a row of colorless homes, each sharing the same white fence, same green lawn, and same paved driveway as the next. A gray haired couple walked a pair of small poodles. Slim white women jogged in spandex shorts. Each person glanced at the two Black kids in tuxedos inside a beige Mercedes. Trevon and I nodded at their grimaced faces, judging smirks, narrow eyes, and acknowledged that we did not belong here.

"Alright bruh, I'ma school you real quick," Trevon said and patted his chest. "You're about to turn eighteen. Since I'm a few months older, I got more experience than you. Like white pussy ain't the best. Sometimes it tastes like carrots. I like carrots and all, but when white pussy gets sweaty and shit, they smell like dog hair. And I can't smash no Asian pussy. Their shit's too tight. And I'm not hating on Black pussy. It's all good when you blowing they back out. BANG. BANG. BANG. But I just can't be dealing with they attitude. And I ain't no racist or sexist because I came out of a Black pussy. Come to think of it, Mexican pussy is the wettest shit ever. But you be worried half the time if you're going to get the bitch pregnant because, well you know, Spanish pussy is like two-hundred percent more fertile than other pussy. I be tripping though, thinking I'm going to get Maria knocked up. Yo, you listening?"

"Yeah," I said. "But all I heard was pussy."

We were approaching a stop sign before the Caldecott tunnel entrance.

The path before me led to prom, but what followed had carried the shadow of home. When I left the house, my parents didn't come back for me. The disbelief gave me more reason to run away from everyone and everything. The farther we drove away, the less sure I was about ever returning home.

"No," I said and lifted my hands from the steering wheel. My foot on the brakes. "No."

"Why you keep saying no, bruh?" Trevon said and pushed my shoulder. "We ain't even close to Taniesha's house, so what you tripping for?"

"My bad, I wasn't thinking." My eyes stared ahead toward the light traffic. My foot stepped on the gas pedal. "Fine, I'm fine."

"You sure?" he asked. "Why don't you let me drive?"

"Hell nah."

"I'm just saying you be in your head too much. What you need to do is loosen up a bit."

I held my breath.

The Mercedes accelerated and entered the tunnel. My eyes focused on the narrow lanes. My mind concentrated on a wish, but this birthday boy didn't deserve a wish. No, a wish didn't make sense on the anniversary of Keon's death. No wish could bring him back to life, but if he could've had a wish, what would my best friend wish for?

I wish, I wish, I wish...

The car drifted farther into the tunnel like one widening vortex. My eyes passed by patterns of glowing yellow lights on gray walls. The air pulled against my lungs. Within the silence, Langston Hughes crept into my mind. He was Keon's favorite poet, the author of his favorite poem, "Teacher." I tried to remember the lines I had copied onto that letter, the same one I had dropped into Keon's burial site:

In this narrow bed of earth,
Stardust never scatters,
I tremble lest the darkness teach
Me that nothing matters.

The tunnel lights turned into a golden blur. The concrete confines, compact cars, and close corners faded in and out of my unclear vision. My breath begged to be free.

"Hey cuckoo," Trevon said and cupped his hands over his mouth. "Bruh, where'd you go? I swear your ass just time traveled or some shit. You listening or what?"

Release. Sunlight lifted my eyelids. My lips parted upon seeing the exit. The Mercedes drove out the tunnel into a red sunset and looming clouds. *Breathe.*

"*Woosah*, whew, wait, what did you say?" I asked.

"Like I was saying," he said and shook his head. "I might end up having to go to Planned Parenthood over that pussy. What about yours? You even know if Taniesha is on any birth-control? I've only been deep in Maria's pussy for like six months. The pussy good and all, but ain't no pussy too good to be no daddy, at least not hers. You listening? What you think?"

"I think you really like the word, pussy."

"Shut your retarded-ass up," he said.

I shook my head. "That word. I don't like it."

Trevon's hands flapped around in a dainty jest. His face squinted. His mouth groaned.

"*I-don't-like-re-tard-ed,*" he teased. "You be on some bullshit, bruh. You don't even realize how much sex we about to get after the prom. I mean, I'm about to be super on one tonight. You ain't even know it."

"I don't know. None of it really matters."

"What you talking about?" he asked and waved his arms. "Pussy is the only thing that matters. Tuxedo, pictures, corsages, hotel, all this shit is for the punany. Like my Uncle J used to say, 'Pussy makes the world go round.' Think, bruh. Why do dudes get haircuts, drive nice cars, wear tight clothes, and work out? I'll tell you why. But first, could I get a drum roll please?"

Trevon tapped his fingers on the dashboard. His voice switched to a sort of deep tenor.

"*Me, me, me, meee, weee dooo it fooor the puuussssy!*"

"Okay, I get it, but can it all be so simple?"

"Bruh, you sounding like Wu-Tang right now, but check it, the whole universe is that simple. I was thinking about this shit the other day in Ethics class. Shit just clicked for me like DING: Life is a porno like living *is* fucking. Think about it, bruh. You watch a porno all the way through, right? Well, sometimes I like to skip to the doggy, but that's beside the point. But you watch it, even though you already know how it's going to end. There's the climax, *that fucking* epiphany moment, whatever you want to call it, then boom, cum shot, *skeet skeet*. That's when the light comes on and everything makes sense. Nobody knows exactly when that shit happens, or how, or what position they going to be in, but it happens. The fucking videos are like our lives, bruh. We're like the actors and actresses, and the millions of genres and websites represent the divisions and subdivisions to our world and shit. Some videos are shorter than others, but they all end the same, more or less."

"We all get fucked," I whispered out the window.

The V-8 engine groaned. Inside the car stood a silence.

A red pickup truck drove past, cutting me off without signaling. Anger rose within my heart, pounding against my chest. My hands clenched the steering wheel. Dr. Imani would always say: *Think before you react.* I avoided honking. The truck decreased speed, forcing me to tailgate. I resisted from rolling down my window and screaming my lungs out. My mind imagined following the driver wherever they were going, jumping out of my car, and beating the person senseless. The truck swerved right past two lanes and then exited off the freeway. I leaned back with a sigh.

"Jonah, you good?" Trevon asked. "Like for real though?"

"Fine, I'm fine," I lied and nodded.

My eyes were focused on the road ahead. Trevon fidgeted in his seat like a restless child. His hand turned on the radio and changed the preset stations repeatedly from N.P.R to KMEL. His fingers played with the bass and tempo level settings, eventually giving up and turning off the radio. His attention switched to his phone, checking his messages, before placing it back into his pocket.

"This silence is killing my vibe, bruh," he said. "I don't like just sitting, and thinking and shit. This car ain't got no bluetooth or nothing?"

"No, I don't know."

"Again with this 'I don't know' shit. Hold up, you still upset our relay team ain't going to State? I don't care what you say. It was Ray's fault for dropping the stick. He's been fucking up ever since he started slanging. You know he popped molly the night before the track meet?"

"I don't care."

"Stop, just stop it already," he said and pointed his finger at my face. "You been acting hella emo since you picked me up. This ain't how I planned to start the night, bruh. Come to think of it, you acting like a straight bitch-ass nigga."

"Don't call me a nigga. I told you not to call me that word."

Trevon grabbed the steering wheel. *Not this.* The entire car jilted from side to side, swerving a few feet into the left lane. *Not now.* My lips pleaded with the air. *Not yet.* Perhaps this was how Keon felt in his last moments out of control, before his car smacked into a tree, before his face cracked onto the steering wheel. *Not me.* I slapped Trevon's hands away and gripped the wheel, keeping the car in steady motion.

"What are you doing?" I shouted. "You crazy?"

"We got to live for the moment," Trevon said. "I mean, think about it. We can wake up tomorrow to a fucking zombie apocalypse, and then what? All we got is just memories. This shit right here is *our* time, but you don't even peep what's about to pop off. Bruh, we in a pussy magnet right now. This CLK is like a mirror on wheels. All these girls see themselves in it. Say it with me, come on now, like Keak da Sneak. *Yadaahmean.*"

Trevon shouted out the window, behaving more wildly than usual. Over the three years I had known him, he had always enjoyed acting as the life of the party, even before the party had begun. During school, Trevon and I would bang on trash cans at lunch time and freestyle to an improvised drum beat. We would post in the hallway and clown anyone who passed by like their shit didn't stink. We would flatter and flirt with the gossiping girls who were as naïve as they were pretty. Trevon and I acted like dumb and dumber until recently when I stopped taking my meds, when I started skipping my therapy, when my illness decided to relive past griefs.

Trevon held his breath, unsnapped his seatbelt, and then propped half his body out the window. He yelled at the passing cars, "*Yaadaameen. Yaadaameen!*"

I clutched onto Trevon's shirt and pulled him inside. He grabbed onto my hand and returned to his seat.

"Get your ass in the car, or I'm not going to bring you," I shouted like my father would.

"What the fuck?" Trevon said and laughed in between catching his breath. He adjusted his seat belt but struggled inserting it into the slot. "I'm just fucking with you, bruh."

"What have you been sipping on?"

"Wait, what, but how'd you know?" he replied.

"Well, from the last party at Ray's, I know you cuss hella much when you're drunk."

"Fuck *yeah*," he said and ignored his seatbelt. He turned around and dug into his duffle-bag in the back seat. He pulled out a Bacardi 151 bottle. "Happy birthday my nig...I mean, my ninja. I got me a fifth of that liquid courage and another unopened one. Plus, I got that 'Get Right' for your b-day, but later though."

"That 'Get Right,' huh?" I asked, shifting glances between the road and Trevon. "Are you sure this gift isn't really for you?"

Trevon shook his head and opened the cap. He raised the bottle close to my nose. My eyes turned watery from the stinging aroma of the Bacardi 151 a.k.a *Gasolina*. I had the flammable alcohol only once at Ray's party around homecoming. My throat felt burnt just from one gulp.

"What's with the no-no-face?" Trevon asked, acting startled. He raised the bottle around my nose again. "Quit acting like a bitch."

"I ain't no bitch, *bitch*," I said and swatted his hand from my face. "I just don't get how your father drinks that stuff."

"Why you always say, father like *fah-ther*, hella proper and shit?" he asked, forcing a smile. His head turned toward the window and let out a sigh. "*Fah-ther* drinks it with coke or mango juice. Some days with his breakfast. Some days with nothing at all. *Fah-ther* blames it on the housing market going to shit, but it's like that for all the real estate agents. He still be yapping on and on about all these mothafuckas moving out of state. He ain't doing shit except complaining. Bruh, I *hate* it when people be putting they burdens on others. Anyway, that reminds me."

Trevon's eyes lit up. He turned around and searched his bag. His hands pulled out two red cups and a Dr. Pepper. The car drove sharply along the curved freeway, causing our bodies to lean to the left. We were near Taniesha's exit.

"Slow down a bit while I do my mixology," Trevon asked and pointed to the 151 between his feet. "Are you going to get in on this?"

"Maybe, I don't know, I guess."

"I don't know if the girls can handle this shit, not even sure you can either, but fuck it. We're about to be fucked up tonight." He reached into his jacket pocket and pulled out a tiny plastic baggy then hid the item within his hand. "Bruh, did I tell you the hotel I booked is like two blocks from the prom? It's about to be paradise in that room like CLAP, CLAP, CLAP, that's the sound of Maria's cheeks like, oh snap, we got to coordinate dips on which bed."

"You've been talking about smashing Maria at the hotel for like a month now. I still don't get why you care so much, but to each his own."

"To eat a bone? Hey, slow down and keep the car steady."

Trevon slouched forward and positioned the cup below the dashboard. He mixed in black soda with the brown 151 into both cups. The carbonated concoction began to make sizzling sounds. He opened the tiny baggy and sprinkled white bits into the drinks. His finger stirred both cups. Within seconds, the baggy had disappeared.

"What was that?"

"What was what?" he said with a devilish grin. "Oh hell nah, I got to keep it one-hundred on why I care so much. You see, I only like my pussy raw. Maria doesn't like that shit, even though her pussy got hella wet when I was teasing her with the tip. Yo, bitches be loving that."

"You're going to get into trouble if you keep that up."

"Nah, but she be on some bullshit, saying she ain't trying to be one of them Mexicanas with a baby in the stroller and a baby in the belly. She's been holding out for like two weeks now, acting hella shady. If I don't get mine tonight, I don't know what I'll do."

"I thought you're supposed to be teaching *me* about pussy."

"So, you a comedian now?" he asked and gave a fake laugh. "I mean, I ain't really sweating it though. If she ain't trying to let me smash, I'm just going to move on to the next one, bruh. Gucci Mane said, 'Girls are like buses, every fifteen minutes one's running.' So there's like a million more chicks than dicks on this planet. These bitches want you to stay with just one of them like that's how God intended. That shit don't make sense. You ask me, that's bad math."

"I don't even believe in marriage anymore," I said with a sudden heaviness sinking in my chest. "For real, I'm not even sure if I'm in love."

"Bruh, why you trying to get all sensitive and shit? I ain't trying to be in my feelings right now. Let's turn up. You're about to be eighteen, and there ain't no cure to the common birthday."

"Wait, where did you learn that?"

"Hey, Taniesha's house is coming up."

"I didn't know you knew where my girlfriend lived."

Trevon studied my blank face for a moment and then returned to his concoctions, examining if they were both evenly split. He looked at the dashboard clock.

"When is Taniesha expecting us?" he asked, ignoring my comment.

"She's been waiting a while. I was supposed to pick her up first. I changed my mind."

"Like you changed your mind about Ray's limo," he said with a smirk. "We lucked out with the Mercedes."

"I was wondering when you were going to bring that up."

"I know Taniesha and them are going to be hella pissed about the limo, and the wait. Girls love to make you wait, but they hate it when you make them wait. Bruh, find somewhere to park before her street. We can pregame before we pregame with the girls."

"The pre-*pre*-game. Alright, fuck it."

"Yeah, that's the Jonah I want to see. And you know I'm about to sneak this 'Get Right' into the prom so we stay lit all night."

The car drove down the off ramp and pulled over at the first street in sight. We parked in a serene neighborhood aligned with redwood houses, manicured lawns, and cropped trees. Trevon handed me the second red cup. I tried keeping it below the view of homes and cars. He tapped his cup against mine. Trevon and I drank in harmony. The cold liquid slithered down my throat. A sharp sting spread throughout my insides.

"And in this narrow bed of earth, stardust never scatters. I tremble lest the darkness teach me that nothing matters," I recited with a grin. Trevon glared. "Ha, I got it right, oh my bad, it's from a poem by Langston Hughes. It was my wish from the tunnel."

"You ain't learned nothing," he said. "Never reveal a wish. Now it won't come true."

CHAPTER 3
MONUMENT

F riday 8:39 p.m.

"We need to talk," Taniesha said.

I watched my girlfriend cross her arms and sit back into the passenger seat. Her smell of discontent and sexiness filled the confines of the Mercedes. Her plump breasts were pushed up against her blue dress top and a bare brown thigh flashed between her slip. Her thin fingers twirled around the neon bracelet that carried the letters: *J-O-N-A-H*. Her frustration intoxicated my senses more than the seven or eight shots of Bacardi

151 from an hour ago. I knew she knew I was drunk. Taniesha was as clever as the devil, but twice as sexy.

"Did you hear me, or are you zoning out again?"

If I had reached for a peek-a-boo down Taniesha's dress, she would've ripped my arm off. My-barely-sober-self resisted the temptation and locked my hands on the steering wheel. My eyes watched the pity sink into my girlfriend's blank stare. As my mama had observed at home, Taniesha also noticed I wasn't feeling like myself tonight. The truth was I hadn't been feeling like myself for a long time.

"Yo babe, yo *baby-babe*, what'd you think about the prom, you know like being at a bank in San Francisco?"

I pointed out the window. She didn't look at the building. Her eyes were focused on me.

"You see what I'm talking about? This place looks like a fucking Greek Temple, a tragedy waiting to happen."

"Jonah," she replied and shook her head. "Look at me for a second."

"Babe, yo *baby-babe*, check out these two mothafuckas acting like they're in love and shit like they got up from a loveseat. He don't love her, not like I…"

"Don't call me *baby-babe*. Listen."

My finger shifted to the direction of Trevon and Maria, both walking together across Sansome and Sacramento Street, a block away from our parked Mercedes. As they marched up the stairs to the Old Federal Reserve building side entrance, Trevon dragged Maria's hand like an adult with a small girl. He had treated her the same way ever since they started dating at the start of the school year. Maria wore her long red gown and black heels but struggled to keep a steady footing up the staircase. Trevon shrugged his shoulders at her and leaned against a tall bronze statue that was easy to recognize, even at night.

"You see that over there!" I shouted and startled Taniesha.

I stared at the statue figure with two human faces as if two separate bodies had joined together. The whole statue was split into multiple slices like a loaf of bread. Trevon and Maria walked past the figure and through a set of concrete columns without a glance at the monument.

"See that statue where Maria almost tripped? It's called, *Hermes and Dionysus: Monument of Analysis*. Dude named Armand Fernandez made it. You see Hermes is on the left. Greeks called him god of transition. He was sending messages and shit between the mortal and immortal worlds. And you see that on the right? It's supposed to be Dionysus, Mista rollercoaster god, the god of drunkenness and joy, god of madness and insanity. Shit, he's probably the same god watching over me. You ever think, hypothetically or what not, that after we die, someone will create a monument for us? I hope it's better than a fucking gravestone with dates and a R.I.P written in bold like they did my best friend. I hated that."

"Dude, you're not listening," Taniesha said.

"I am listening."

"No, you're not. I can tell."

She pointed at my chest with her annoying index finger. A gesture my mama often did to my father. A gesture Trevon would often do while I drove. A gesture Taniesha knew would set me off. In spite of her actions, I could only control my own reactions.

"Wait, you don't believe me about the statue, huh? I read about it in the S.F Chronicle. It's symbolic for like the disintegration of life being healing, and transforming is like the return to life, or something like that."

"I don't care about the stupid statue. We need to talk."

"I thought we were talking."

"No, you're talking. So, talk about this, why did you think that joke would be funny?"

"What are you talking about?"

"You know exactly what I'm talking about."

Taniesha watched and waited like a tigress about to pounce onto her prey. Her body didn't move from her seat or utter another sound. We both sat in the Mercedes, playing the waiting game. She waited for me to admit a blurred truth while under liquid courage. I waited to recall the joke she was referring to. Although people love making jokes, no one loved being the punch-line, my eyes looked away to avoid her lie detector glare. I noticed the Old Federal Reserve staircase was empty. Trevon and Maria had entered the prom gates. My mind imagined the inside of prom: bright strobe lights, fake red-carpet, time-themed props, clock-decorated tables. At the center of it all were my so-called friends, asking why the hell were Jonah and Taniesha waiting in the car on the greatest night of their lives.

"Wait, you don't remember, huh?" she asked. "Damn, it was only like an hour ago. Tre knocked on the door, pretending he was you. He was like, 'Hi, I'm Jonah.' He was holding the white corsage in his hand, the same one I picked out. My mama asked about your father, and Tre really said, 'He's good, work is fine.' She believed he was you, since she never met you before."

"Damn, I don't remember shit," I replied.

"Did you tell him to do all of that stuff?"

"I told him some of it. I don't know. We were both drunk."

"Damn right you're drunk. And the worst part was when we were taking pictures with Maria's family, you kept making those stupid shitty faces. I mean, eight-year-olds act more mature than you. And when my daddy figured it out, oh no, he didn't like it, not one bit. He told me, he wasn't going to let me go out at first, but he knew some 'good folks' who worked with your father at the courthouse, so it was like whatever after that."

"You look so sexy when you're angry."

"Is that why you enjoy making me upset?"

Taniesha rubbed the neon bracelet. Her body froze. Only her fingers moved and traced the lettering. When the motions felt no more relief, my girlfriend let out a sigh and gazed out the open window. Just like me, she was lost between her mind and heart.

"I'm so sorry Taniesha, really," I admitted.

"*Really?*" she repeated. "If you had said one more thing about Dionysus, I would have *really* thrown this damn thing out the window. I don't care if it's *really* your birthday."

She removed the bracelet and squeezed it tight in her palm.

"I'll stop, that's it, okay," I said, but couldn't resist. "For real though, it's just fucked up how Fernandez mixed both gods like that, like man and god are one in the same. I ain't no god. You ain't god. I mean yeah, transitions and insanity are all the same shit, but you can't be the life of the party and a life for change, that's like to say...what the fuck?"

Taniesha had thrown the bracelet out the window. The mini neon colors soared into the dark street like a glowing fast ball. She leaned back in her seat and pointed at me with her index finger again.

"Really?"

I unlocked the door and sprinted out the car, nearly cramping my left thigh from the rush of adrenaline. I stopped in the middle of Sansome Street and searched the barely lit concrete for a $9.99 piece of beads and string. A stretch limo flashed bright headlights, driving slowly toward me. Not a single glimmer of a brake-light. I jumped onto the curb, seconds before the bumper approached my foot. The limo rolled by like a long black hearse on a night call. Cheers and curses screamed from the cracked tinted window.

"Are you okay?" Taniesha shouted from the Mercedes.

"Oh, now you're worried?"

I exhaled a deep groan, walking with vigilance into the street. I turned on the flash-light app to my phone and found the bracelet hidden within the white lines. The stitching material was still in the same worn condition as the bracelet on my wrist. My name was as clear as night.

"Don't ever do that again," she said and opened the driver's side door, waving her hand.

"Don't make me do that again," I said and returned to the car. "I almost died for you."

"Nobody should die for anybody," she replied and shook her head.

I laid the bracelet in her palm. Her brown cheeks lifted and her mouth shined a row of white. This was the calm face I had seen nearly nine months ago when I gave her the gift. She didn't care that the two custom bracelets were from a cheap souvenir store. She only cared that we shared something intimate and special. The bracelet she placed back on her wrist was more than a discounted souvenir. The gift was a reminder our hearts were never alone.

"We got these at the Marina, on our first date. You wore that yellow sundress. Damn, you looked fine, like art in motion. Do you remember us sharing the Baskin Robbins?"

"You remember leaning in for a kiss?" she asked, grinning from ear to ear. Small giggles escaped out her mouth. "And you remember when those seagulls dropped a load of shit on your shoulder?"

"Yeah, I remember they unloaded 24-hours of diarrhea on my fresh cardigan. That shit was new too. My mama said, 'There ain't a spot that bleach can't fix,' but I ended up throwing that stanky thing away. There's some shit you just can't rub off."

"Probably for the best. You looked like Carlton in that thing anyway. I thought you were going to break out in his dance at any moment."

Within an instant, we both gyrated our bodies, swayed our arms, and snapped our fingers. "The Carlton dance" was a routine whenever our favorite scenes of *Fresh Prince of Bel-Air* came on TV. Before our honeymoon phase ended. Before our happy bubble began to burst.

"*Duh, dun-dun, duh, dun-dun,*" I sang into an invisible mic in my hand. Tom Jones' spirit had taken over my body. "*It's not unusual to be loved by anyone.*"

We laughed. Our voices carried a harmony that lasted longer than the minute it filled.

"I'll never forget our first date, for better or worse," she said.

"It's like all we have are our memories, but it's all for the best like Voltaire would say."

"Yes, all for the best," she repeated with a contagious smile. "See that was sweet, but I can't tell if you're being serious or not. You've been acting hella weird lately like you've been going from zero to a hundred. Is it because of the full moon?"

"There's something I have to tell you," I said super seriously. "*I'm not like other guys.*"

"Wait, what's that from...*Thriller*? Do I look like I got a jheri-curl?"

She let out a short *hee-hee* and then pushed my shoulder.

"Dude, let's be real. Your moods are like hella up and down. I be worried and kinda scared, even when you say, 'Fine, I'm fine,' like hella weird and shit."

"You sound like my mama right now."

"You mean the mama I only met once," she said and paused.

Taniesha sat in silence and stared into the night. Her bare shoulders shivered from the cool breeze. Her hands fiddled with the lock button and door handle, attempting to break free.

"Are you cold?" I rolled up her window. "How do you really feel?"

"No, I don't know, no," she mumbled and then released her grip on the door. "It's just that sometimes, I don't know, I don't think you love me."

"Here we go again."

A thousand tiny prickles raced along my arms, climbed my shoulders and neck, and crawled on my face. My lips felt pinched with the urge to admit: *I love you Taniesha, ever since we shared Bio class together, but loving you means trusting that you must know the truth like my parents are getting a divorce, today is the anniversary of my best friend's death, and I've been off my meds for longer than I should have, you see, I want to love you Taniesha, but I don't love myself.* Such words in my head that were never said. My eyes opened wide, glancing back and forth between Taniesha and the statue.

"Where'd you go?" she asked. "Were you listening?"

My mind was running a mile a minute, yet my body was still in the present. I nodded and pointed at the statue.

"If I were a god, I wouldn't want that mess dedicated in my honor. It didn't belong here, neither did we because we aren't idols, only ideals."

"Sheesh," Taniesha interrupted. "Do you love me?"

"No wait, it's like the poem I told you about. Yeah, Hughes predicted everything when he said, *'Ideals are like the stars, always above our reach,'* almost like he was saying there ain't no point to it all like we're all just a bunch of..."

"No Jonah, do you love me?" she repeated, more seriously.

"What'd you say?"

"Listen Jonah, just listen, do...you...love me? Why is it so hard for you to say it?"

"But a hundred hearts are still too few to carry the amount of love I have for you."

"Stop with the stupid quotes, and just be honest for once. You only say, 'I love you' when I say it first, or when you want to get in my panties."

"No, I say it all the time. I love you, I love you Taniesha. I guess, I don't know for sure, but I'm damn sure, I almost got hit by a car trying to get a bracelet. Why do we have to talk about this right now?"

"Nobody's around," she said and pointed toward the monument. "Everyone is inside already, enjoying the prom, *our* prom, and they're probably hella lit by now. Problem is we're alone here, and you can't tell me what's really going on. If there's anyone you can talk to, it's your girlfriend. You know we've been together long enough to have a child?"

I hated talking about kids, birth, and making life. We were only high school seniors, yet we had discussed the possibility of a family at least three times within our relationship. Taniesha had forgotten to mention that humans spent nine months in a womb, completely absent of light. She didn't realize that some people carried about their daily lives in constant fear of darkness. Not Taniesha though. She couldn't fear something she didn't know.

"We talked about this before."

"But you always give different reasons."

"I don't want another Tarver to go through the same bullshit as my father, and his father, and probably my father's father's father. No, my legacy has to be something better. No, it will be something deserving of ah, ha-ha, fucking monument."

I watched a waterfall of tears flow down Taniesha's cheeks. Her make-up smeared, yet she still appeared like a Black Barbie doll sitting inside a luxury car. Her puppy-dog eyes, caramel brown complexion, dark mahogany hair, and sky blue dress gave an illusion of a happy world. She would never understand my loneliness.

"Are you ready to go in?" she asked.

Taniesha used a wet wipe to clean her running mascara. She blew her nose and tossed the wipe out her window. She rattled her cup and grunted.

"I want to drink some of the 151," she ordered. "Anymore Dr. Pepper left for chase?"

"I think Trevon and Maria drank it all, but they snuck some inside. You can drink what's left of mine, but I think Trevon might've mixed it up with something. Wait, what was all that you said yesterday? You remember, 'Oh, I'm not going to drink or take anything because I want to remember everything.' You know what Seneca said, 'Drunkenness is nothing else but voluntary madness.' Actually, never mind. That didn't save him from killing himself."

"Just shut up, shut up already!" she shouted. "You still don't get it, do you?"

I watched my girlfriend drop her shoulders and reach for my red cup.

"I want to get drunk. I don't want to talk."

CHAPTER 4
PRESSURE

F riday 9:40 p.m.

"How long have the girls been in the bathroom?" I asked Raynold. He sat across the table more quieter than a meditating monk. "Why you think they always go with someone to the bathroom? Do you think it's like safety in numbers?"

"They go to talk," Raynold replied and rolled his eyes.

"Talk about what?"

"The Bible, their period," he said. "How the fuck should I know?"

I watched the Black six-foot-three basketball/track star, drug-dealer, senior shrug his broad shoulders as if he could care less. Raynold took a long gulp from his glass of water. Drips spilled from his trimmed beard onto his white tuxedo collar. He slammed the glass on the round table and turned his tall frame away from my direction. His attention shifted toward the fancy-dressed fakes inside the bank hall.

My peers stood around the dance floor like a herd of privileged gazelles near a pond. The athletes, preppies, and self-proclaimed "pretty girls" gathered in packs, each dressed in various hipster-like suits and barely-legal fitted gowns. Above them hung a spinning disco ball that illuminated their on-and-off beat motions. They texted. They selfied. They performed multi-stepped handshakes and synchronized owl chants. They did everything possible to hide and cover their present reality of unhappiness. Maybe Raynold knew how pointless everything truly was, or perhaps he knew nothing like everyone else.

"I don't know why Tre went with the girls," I said. "You think they're talking about us?"

"Why do you give a fuck?" Raynold replied. "Ain't like you went with them anyway."

"Chillax." I extended my hand. He was out of reach. "You didn't go either."

"At least me and Sasha took the limo with the others," he said. "I'm still heated, bruh. We were planning this whole prom thing for months. We were supposed to be all in on the limo, then you just cat on us last minute.

I don't like no flakes, but I guess, that's just who you is, huh?"

"Okay, so that's why you're upset? Like I said on the phone, it was just a change of plans. Don't get all butt hurt. My father let me borrow his Mercedes at the last minute."

"Nah bruh, I'm not butt hurt, but you just be thinking about yourself. Not giving a fuck about nobody else."

"That's not true. So, what do you want? Me apologize again?"

His head shook twice. "It's whatever nigga."

Raynold shrugged his broad shoulders and turned his back towards me again like a stubborn child. He was ignoring me on purpose. So I decided to distract myself on purpose. My fingers slid around the rim of my cold glass, trying to cast a spell to change the water to wine. I hated the bitter taste of vino, but I would have taken anything at that point. My buzz was wearing off. My half-filled glass was aligned with the others set on our satin linen table.

Why are they all full except for mine?

A bouquet of white roses sat at the center surrounded by six black candles. The fresh flowers rested inside a vase shaped like a round clock. By next morning, the decorations of my peers' delusions would be thrown away as either compost or recyclable. This decorative dump was like everyone and everything connected to my presence: Pointless.

The longer I sit still, the more I want to leave.

Three Black dudes in flashy red tuxedos appeared from the back and immersed into the mixed crowd on the dance floor. The three formed a triangular circle, pushing aside bodies, clearing an open space for a crowd to form and surround them at the center. Each wannabe dancer took his turn to show off a couple seconds of break moves and pop-locks. The crowd hooted. A group of girls hollered. Someone chanted, "GO, GO, GO!"

Trevon appeared from the mass of teenage bodies, mingling with several on-lookers. His snorting laughs somehow carried over the crowd's shouting voices, and even broke through the deep bass of Keak Da Sneak's song, "That's my word" playing from the corner speakers. Trevon joined the three boys, poorly imitating their motions like a drunken fool. He was just another character in this grand scheme. In this narrow bed of earth, life was a play. We were mere players and props. What mattered was the excellence of the acting. I didn't belong on this stage.

"It's a bunch of niggas out there," Raynold said, breaking the silence. He tugged on the table linen and pointed at the black candles. "Niggas ruin shit for everyone."

"When you say it like that, you sound kinda racist."

"Racism requires power; therefore, Black people can't be racist, nigga."

"I hate the n-word."

"Bruh, it's just a word. It's only weird when white folks and bougie negros say it. Besides, I heard your dad's a judge. Don't he give jail sentences to niggas?"

"He passes sentences to all kinds of people."

"But most of them people are niggas, right?"

He paused for my reply. I nodded twice as a frown weighed down his brown face.

"Are you even from the Town?" he asked. "Have you ever been to a sideshow? I mean come on bruh, why you didn't just go to a private school?"

"Damn, when did this turn into an interrogation? For one, I was born and raised in Oakland, but that decision wasn't on me. And two, my father would kill me if he caught me doing donuts. And three, my parents wanted my brother and I to have the 'public school experience' like them. They wanted us not to become hella bougie, unlike them, even though my mama's a R.N. But what's up with all the questions?"

"My Uncle Al died last year on the job. He was like most firemen and didn't do anything wrong, just saving cats and old people. He was a *good* Black man. But it don't matter anyway. There's good people, and then, there's niggas. You see Jonah, I'm cool with you. Aside from track and the bullshit you pulled tonight, I like you, believe it or not. You ain't no nigga though, but you be doing nigga shit. You ever watch Chris Rock? He said it's the niggas who are ruining everything for everybody. Them the ones holding us back."

"I always thought there was something bigger."

"Nah, it's like nigga genocide," he said. "Fuck all that Black Lives Matter shit. More niggas killing Blacks than cops. Them the savages fucking up society. You remember that pimp out in West Oakland last month? You know, the one who got locked up for pouring Drain-O down that Black hooker's throat? He was the same nigga who beat that Black tranny to death. Come on bruh, it's cold-blooded devils like that who be messing up shit for everybody. Them the *real* niggas."

"Sorry, you never told me about your uncle. What happened to him?"

"He was killed. Just shot and robbed on the job by a bunch of niggas."

"Damn, damn, it's like that one saying, 'Apathy is living oblivion,' you know?" I nodded, but he looked back quizzically. "I mean, I'm so sorry."

"I don't feel sorry for niggas." He pointed at my chest. "You shouldn't feel sorry either."

"Why you keep repeating it when I told you I hate that word? I always have."

"The word ain't the problem."

"What's the problem then?"

Trevon approached our table. He was singing to himself.

"You gon' be a dope fiend, your friends should call you dopey. Keep my names out they mouth 'cause they don't know me. I wish, I wish I could fuck every girl in the wooorrrrld!"

Though completely off-key, Trevon stretched the final notes to Young Money's song, "Every girl in the world," as though he was Luciano Pavarotti rapping the

Lil' Wayne lyrics in an Italian opera. He swayed his arms rhythmically like a conductor leading an orchestra. He gradually lost his breath. Once he collected himself, he sat in the empty chair facing Raynold.

"I love me some Lil' Wayne," Trevon said. "Top five alive, my nigga. All of Wayne's shit comes straight from the dome, and hella bitches be on his jock. When I grow up, I'ma be just like him, rich with hella babymamas. Matter of fact, folks were talking in the bathroom about the whole upper floor being empty. I'm going to take Maria's fat-ass up there, and '*watch me back it up and dump it, back, back it up and dump it.*' Y'all know what I'm saying."

"You hella on one already," Raynold said. "Just don't forget about our other shit."

I sat at the table between my two friends wasting away like everyone else. If I had left, no one would look for me. My obligation was bound to Taniesha. Even that excuse was losing weight without her presence around. When I entered the Old Federal Reserve building earlier, the exit was the first idea in my mind. Nothing else mattered. Not the two tall gray arches. Not the hallway's narrow mouth. Not the Flava-Flav-like clocks mounted on the walls. Not the black and white banner with the word 'TIMELESS' covered in sprinkles, all of which were bullshit. These people knew nothing about time. They used time worse than anything.

When their clock is nearly up, time is what they will want most.

"You're zoning out again," Trevon said and shook my shoulder. "How come you ain't go with me and the girls to the bathroom? We got our drank on."

"Why does it matter? I'm over drinking." I said.

"You ain't trying to get fucked up?" Trevon asked. "You missed out on getting more of my 'Get Right.' The girls finished it all, but Maria was acting like a B-I-A, B-I-A, and not trying to take a swig. I don't know what's her problem, but she better not be on her period. If so, I'ma tell her not to. They still in the bathroom, doing their make-up, probably cleaning their pussies and shit. All of them are hella on one. I'm already feeling myself too. I just need that last ingredient."

Trevon and Raynold traded glances from across the table, without once looking at me.

"I thought we were going to wait until at the hotel?" Raynold asked. "Don't you pull a 'Jonah' right now."

"What's that supposed to mean?"

"I ain't changing my mind last minute," Trevon said and laughed.

He looked around the room, and flashed some folded cash to Raynold before retracting back to his pocket.

"Nah bruh, right now while the girls are still in the bathroom," Trevon said.

"I got joog on these skittles," Raynold said.

He pulled out a plastic sandwich bag and pressed it to his lips. He sucked the air out of it, sealed it shut, and hid it below the table.

"Shit's pure," Raynold said. "None of that Special K shit. Twenty a pop. This batch is better than that shit from before. It'll hit sooner, last longer, and the crash is only half as bad."

"You sound like one of those 5-hour energy drinks," Trevon said with a smirk. "I was thizzing for like twelve hours last time I popped. Then I found out that shit was mixed with some Special K. On God bruh, I almost died."

"What's Special K? K like ketamine? What are you guys doing?"

"If you have to ask, then you're not down," Raynold said.

"Did you know ecstasy was once used to treat stuttering?" Trevon stated with pride.

"No, I didn't know that, thanks Mr. Teacher," I told Trevon and turned to Raynold. "Was that why folks at your party were chewing on straws all night?"

"You don't want your teeth looking like you gnawing on rocks," Raynold said and opened his mouth to flash his braces. "What's with all the questions?"

"Yo, hook my student up," Trevon ordered.

"I mean, you are about to turn eighteen in a few hours," Raynold said and glanced at the wall clock. "And there still ain't no cure to the common birthday."

"I swear, I heard that before. But I never tried that stuff. Neither has Taniesha, I think."

"You think she'll want to take a hit?" Trevon asked. "Would you ever spike her drink?"

"Whoa man, I'm not trying to rape her."

"Nah bruh, I didn't mean it like that," he said with an odd smile. "Just sometimes, when they ain't feeling it, you need to help them get loose and relaxed."

"That sounds like rape."

"Nah bruh, it's not like that," Trevon said and waved up his hands in defense. "When you a dude and it hits, you be rock hard for hours like your dick and balls just turned into Pinocchio's nose, or face. I forgot the story."

"I don't know, that still sounds like rape," Raynold said. Small cries of laughter crept out his mouth. "And come on nigga, this shit ain't Viagra. Why you need help with your dick already? What you going to do when you like thirty? I bet your shit will probably shrivel up by then like a little pickle."

"Man, shut yo bitch-ass up," Trevon said and nearly jumped out of his chair.

Raynold sat back in his seat and crossed his arms.

"Nah, my dick ain't no dill pickle," Trevon said and pointed at Raynold's glaring eyes. "My shit's a cucumber with the bun, on God. Nah, my shit is a navy ship, and all these bitches want my seamen. Just ask your mama, bruh. She checked the deck this morning."

"Oh, we're going into mamas now," Raynold said. His eyes flared up like the first stages of a Super-Saiyan. "Don't let me *ether* you right now, you one pump nigga. Remember I ain't sold you no shit yet." He moved his chair closer to mine. "Are we doing this or what?"

"I don't know," I admitted and breathed deeply.

Two pairs of eyes were sizing me up from my seat. They no longer saw a peer. A desperate boy had appeared. My tolerance withered thin from the pressure.

"I never tried it before. I'm not good with pills, or any drugs for that matter."

"Look, ain't nobody forcing you to do anything," Raynold said. "If you want to be like a hermit and stay in your shell all the time then go ahead. Hermits don't deal with peer pressure."

"That was the only thing I learned in Bio class," Trevon said.

"We're wasting hella time," Raynold said and nudged Trevon's arm. He pointed to the plastic bag resting in his lap. "I got mine. You got yours?"

They nodded simultaneously.

"What happened to all that 'holding us back' talk?" I asked Raynold.

"Holding *who* back?" Trevon interrupted.

"Nah, you trying to say I'm a hypocrite?" Raynold asked and bit his lip. His voice grew tense. "Don't give me that bullshit, when you made me, Marquise, Patrick, and Kenny pay for the limo cut that *y'all* flaked on. Just another hundred out of my pocket, right?"

"Chillax, man," I said.

"Everybody not balling like you, Jonah. We ain't got rich-ass parents like you, Jonah. You the one fucking lying to folks and being the hypocrite, Jonah, so don't come at me with that bullshit, bruh."

"I told you already I was sorry," I said and extended my hand. He declined. "Really?"

"Honestly, I was just following Jonah," Trevon told Raynold.

"Honestly?" Raynold repeated, shaking his head. "Y'all are just some selfish-ass niggas."

"Don't do me like that bruh," Trevon said. "We're all in the same boat. My pockets are thin too. I needed to save a little because I'm really pushing it with the Marriott room."

"Are we still going to do this or what?" Raynold asked. "You too busy talking."

Raynold moved his chair closer to Trevon's. He kept his hands below the table, holding what appeared to be a bag of color-coated pills. Trevon accepted the bag and exchanged a stack of folded cash held together by a red paper clip. Both players counted their earnings. Their faces glowed with satisfaction, oblivious to the huge stage around them.

"On all honest virtues, I sought to keep firm hold."

"On all what?" Raynold asked and looked up.

"Pay him no mind," Trevon told Raynold. "He was saying the same mumbo jumbo shit when we were in the car. He's like that Black granny in *The Matrix*. Next thing he'll do is start bending spoons and shit. Bruh, we should watch the Matrix tomorrow, and get some Chipotle."

"Nah, I can't eat that shit again," Raynold said. "You remember last time we ate the chicken bowl and got the bubble-guts? Them B.Gs ain't no joke."

"Who you telling? After we ate that shit, I was just trying to stay alive my nigga."

"Sorry to interrupt, but I was just thinking," I said. "So like if I took it, what if I cut it in half? Maybe I can do a smaller dose since I don't like pills."

"What are you going to do with the rest?" Raynold asked.

"I don't know."

"If you're going to go into the water, you might as well dive balls deep into the ocean."

"But I don't know how to swim."

"Me neither," Trevon said with a sigh.

"Am I the only Black person who can swim?" Raynold said. "I guess I have to teach y'all how to swim this summer, just in case the ice caps melt. Niggas don't own any boats."

"At least we have ladders," Trevon shouted.

"Heads up," Raynold warned like he saw a bear. He adjusted his pockets and turned to Trevon. "Here come the girls. I don't want them to know how much we got. Put your shit away."

Our three dates approached the table, each one gift-wrapped within a vibrant dress. The girls paraded their curvy bodies through the narrow pathways. Taniesha led in the middle in her sky blue dress. On the right was Sasha dressed in bright green. On the left was Maria dressed in passion red. The teen beauty queens bumped against nearly everyone and everything in their path. They giggled like wild hyenas and waved their manicured claws at the sight of our greetings. Once they reached our seats, their laughter and chanting had already filled the void left by our voluntary silence.

"Hey boys," Sasha said and stood behind Raynold. "Did you miss us?"

"I grew a beard since you've been gone," Raynold said.

"Oh snap, I love Kelly Clarkson!" Maria shouted and threw her arms into the air. She leaned into Trevon and began to sing. *"Since you've been gone, I can breathe for the first time, I'm moving on, yeah yeah, since you..."*

"You killing me," Trevon said. His hands smacked the table. "That song is hella-ela old."

"Sooorrrry," Maria said and swung her arms in protest. "I thought you liked my singing."

An awkward silence settled upon the table. Maria's high-yellow face grew rosy from embarrassment. I stood up and switched my seat so Maria could sit next to Trevon. Maria sat down with a sigh of relief. Sasha followed and sat next to Raynold. Taniesha stood still, watching and waiting. Her mouth turned downwards as her brown eyes pierced mine. She noticed I wasn't moving. She pulled her seat out and sat down across from Trevon.

"Are you going to act like I'm not here?" Taniesha said and crossed her arms.

"Sorry," I whispered. "I wasn't thinking, I mean, sorry, my bad."

Everyone looked at me and then they looked at her.

"Soooo," Raynold said. He raised his pinky finger to his chin. "I was just wondering, why do girls go to the bathroom in groups?"

"All women are sworn to secrecy," Sasha said. Her finger traced a cross over her heart.

"Bullshit," Trevon said. "I can Google it right now and know why in like thirty seconds."

"I bet I can guess what you guys were talking about," Taniesha said, still looking at me.

"You can't figure it out," Trevon said. "But just to be fair, we'll give you three guesses." "Was it sex?" Taniesha replied effortlessly. "It was probably drugs, or sports, or having sex on drugs while playing sports."

"Was that three guesses?" Trevon asked.

"But wait, we talk about other stuff too," I said. "We are creatures capable of depth."

"What else did you talk about then?" Taniesha asked.

"If you really want to know, we were trying to keep the party going," Raynold said.

Everyone saw him pat Sasha's butt. He pulled on her arm. She submitted with ease and leaned closer into his lap.

"If you keep that going baby, you're going to find another surprise," Raynold said.

"Stop playing around," Sasha said and sat up. She adjusted her perm black hair. "Come on daddy, can I get a pop please?"

"Okay, y'all want to pop some molly?" he asked and looked at Taniesha and Maria.

"I never did it before," Maria admitted.

"Yeah, me too," Taniesha said. "I'm kind of buzzing already from all the shots Tre gave us. He still didn't tell me what was in it."

"That 'Get Right' special," Trevon said. "Now are you girls trying to get turnt up?"

"Are you going to pop too?" Maria asked Trevon. "I'll do it if Taniesha does it."

"I don't know," Taniesha said, looking around the table. "Jonah, are you going to try it?"

One hundred eyes stared at me all at once. My pulse danced. My heart drummed. The air thickened. My vision blurred. My body declined to cry, or scream, or run. Each passing millisecond pushed my will deeper into helplessness. My chair was sinking into the floor, or was I sinking into my chair?

I watched Trevon's fingers *tap, tap, tap* on the table, interrupting the silence of the lambs. My best friend raised his half-filled glass of water in the air then cleared his throat.

"I've said this before whenever we go hard. Ray knows, so he can co-sign. This ain't one of those *everyone's-jumping-off-a-bridge-so-you-do-it-too* kind of moments. You can leap with the rest of us, if you want, or you can stay where you at, on the edge. But once you start seeing us flying high and soaring through the sky and shit, just know you lost your chance."

"That has no meaning, at all," Taniesha said. "What about when you finally land?"

"Sheesh, everything has meaning," Raynold said and looked in my direction. "But nothing really matters once you taste the rainbow. So, what are you going to do?"

CHAPTER 5
WALTZ

F riday 10:20 p.m.

"One, two, three, and one, two, three, you almost got it," Taniesha instructed me. "You see, it's simple like one, two, three, and one, two, three."

"Nothing's that simple," I said and shook my head in disappointment.

At the center of the bank hall, my girlfriend swayed with grace in spite of her tight fitted blue dress. Her curvy body moved easily from side to side. Underneath the disco ball, glimmers of absolution radiated from her brown skin. Her careful steps carried the elegance of a ballerina in high heels. I watched her flowing movements, feeling frustrated my feet couldn't do the same.

"You know dancing ain't really my thing," I said.

"Come on, don't give up," she pleaded and touched my face. "You see, it's one, two, three like we practiced at Maria's quinceañera. Dude, you got this."

"Dude, look around."

I pointed to an Asian girl next to us. She was bent over in the three-point stance. A tall lanky white boy was on the receiving end, groping her backside. Slowly, her white skirt slid up her thighs.

"Now you see. Everyone is twerking."

"Okay, but you started waltzing first," she said and stopped mid-dance. "Now follow along. Tell me, what's the count?"

I scratched my head as if confused. "Hmm, let me guess. Is it one, two, and a three?"

"Yay, you're learning," she said and blew a kiss into the air. My hand flew up, caught her kiss, and brought it to my heart. Then she smiled from ear to ear. "You're so corny. That's why I love you. Now let's keep trying. Don't give up on me."

Taniesha could never resist a moment to teach me a lesson. My girlfriend placed my hand on her waist and squeezed my fingers to follow. She took her first step forward. Left to right. Forward then left. Backwards then right. She clicked both heels together, completing the square. Finally, she clapped twice and concluded the dance tutorial.

"And one, two, three, that's it babe. How do you feel?" She smiled and held my waist to align with hers. "Your body needs to get into it like real *nat-ur-al*, you know. Try not to think too much, and dude, don't stare at my feet. It's weird."

"But I can't dance sober."

Her brown face glowed under the disco ball. Her disarming smile left me with no other choice but to comply. My body continued imitating her motions, at the same time, repeating her directions in my head. I took my first step forward like an anxious toddler.

"Alright, I can do this. I can be normal."

Left. Right. Forward. Left. Backwards. Right.

Our feet matched each step. Our motions flowed together. Our bodies swayed in-sync to the beat. The enchantment of our dance binded our spirits as if two lives formed one force.

"Bruh, stop staring at my feet," Taniesha said with a low voice.

"Don't say *bruh*," I said and returned my attention to her smile. "It doesn't sound right when you say it."

"Oh, like it sounds right when y'all say it like all the time."

"Wait, I can't believe it," I said and clapped, finally waltzing with my girlfriend.

"Yay, I knew you had rhythm. I was about to question your Blackness."

"What'd you mean? I'm Wesley Snipes Black. But you can't ask for rhythm when it comes to a sugar plum fairy waltz. Did you see any Black people dancing in the Nutcracker?"

"I don't think I've ever seen it before. Do you remember how it ends?"

"I remember it ends like all stories end."

With each blinking moment, forgotten memories flashed from another time. Last Christmas morning. Cinnamon waffles covered in cut strawberries. Cheddar cheese scrambled eggs. Pigs-and-a-blanket. Everything stacked and spread onto four plates. My mama had cooked a grand breakfast. Steven sat on the couch, one hand twirling his Captain America action figure, the other holding his cup of hot cocoa. My father was busy finishing legal work in his home office, as usual. I remembered running upstairs in excitement, humming and knocking the "two bits" tune onto his door, *dah-di-di-dah-di, di-di,* only to have been told, "Tell your mother to start without me this time." Only my mama, little brother, and I had opened presents in the family room. The three of us posed to take pictures. The three of us ate breakfast at the dining table. The three of us gathered on the couch to watch Carroll Ballard's *Nutcracker.* I remembered last Christmas day because by the end of watching the film, my father had finally joined the three of us, only to have told the family: "I'm sorry for everything."

My eyes opened.

"Jonah, are you okay?" Taniesha asked.

Her fingers caressed my cheek. Her affection brought me back to the present.

"Where'd you go? Talk to me," she said.

"Fine, I'm fine," I lied.

My hand touched hers, slowly removing her warmth from my cold body. Her hand retreated to her side. We continued our waltz.

"Okay, now I remember the Nutcracker. The rat king died. Then there was this sugar plum fairy thingy acting like the H.B.I.C of Candyland. The main girl and her prince-charming got hella turnt up from waltzing. So, they were just waltzing and waltzing until she danced herself to sleep. Then she woke up to find out the dude was just a toy, you know, like that stupid-ass Pinocchio. Finally, she got shook and was like, 'God damn, I was dreaming the whole time.' The end. Happily ever after, I guess, whatever that means."

"I guess, we can skip the play," she said and shrugged her shoulders.

Our bodies commenced an almost robotic waltz. My eyes retreated from Taniesha's gaze and stared across the dim bank hall. Our reserved table was empty. All six chairs were pulled out of place. A few feet away were Raynold and Sasha dancing the two-step and pretending Taniesha and I were invisible. My so-called "friends" stood in between my former track teammates, Patrick, Marquise, Kenny, and their chatty freshmen dates. Due to my limo mistake, their sharp stares and petty glares saw me as a flake. They would rather cut off my nose in spite of my face.

A tall lanky white boy and his date appeared out of nowhere and walked up behind Raynold. The boy wore the ugliest white-and-black-Tony-Montana-rip-off-suit I had ever seen. Him and Raynold shook hands, their fingers partially closed. They grasped each other's palms before eventually letting go with something in their hands. The white boy nodded and walked away toward a Latino couple holding red cups and straws. The exchange went unnoticed by those around them.

"Hold up," Taniesha said, her face riddled with confusion. "What were you implying with all that stuff about the Nutcracker?"

"I don't imply anything."

"Liar liar."

"Prove it then."

"Maybe I can if we see a show later this year, when we're back from winter break."

"I haven't thought that far."

"I think Syracuse and Long Beach State are on the same schedules but, and this is kind of a big but, our whole long-distance thing. You know, some folks say out of sight, out of mind."

"Even when or if you're out of sight, you're still all I see."

I smiled. Her brown cheeks lifted and tiny dimples sprouted on her face.

"I think I'm blushing, and you know Black people don't blush," she said. "But for real, we haven't really talked about the long-distance relationship. It's almost like you've been ignoring it or something."

"Ignoring facts makes them go away," I said with a smile and wink. "Hey, let's just dance, okay. One, two, three."

Our bodies continued in a full robotic waltz. My ears ignored her heavy sigh. My eyes observed the rest of the bank hall. My stare locked onto Ms. Sexton, often mispronounced as Ms. Sexting, who carried a measuring tape. The middle-aged brunette strutted onto the dance floor dressed in a white blouse, navy-blue pencil skirt, and black pumps like a sexy librarian on her way to start some drama. Several students stepped back, clearing a path for the Assistant Principal as though she was Moses parting the Red Sea.

Within seconds, Ms. Sexton approached a close-knit couple in mid-twerk and separated the boy and girl. She pulled on her measuring tape, stretching a length of about two feet as advised within the prom conduct agreement. I could read her lips, lecturing the embarrassed couple about what I assumed was "the dignified space between respectable partners." When she left to continue her inspections, the couple flipped her off and began chewing on plastic straws.

"Yo, what up seniors," the D.J said over the microphone.

The music dissolved. Groups of chatter faded into whispers and faint noises.

"I said, what up SENIORS!" he shouted again, inciting everyone to scream. "How y'all feeling out there? This is D.J Amen serving the tunes for the room. We're still taking song requests. This next one is from James and goes out to Maya. He said, 'Each moment with you is like a dream to me that somehow came true.' Alright, I see you sampling the great Rod Temperton. We're going to take it back with some Heatwave y'all. Now all the lovely couples get to the dance floor, and don't make me point some of y'all out."

I watched Ms. Sexton retreat to the prom entrance and positioned herself between Assistant Principal Haley, Mr. Garcia who was the security guard, and a short Asian girl from the Leadership club. They checked in students from the lobby through a three-tiered scanning process: At the front stood Mr. Haley in his red checkered suit who reviewed the ticket information and I.D cards. Next, Mr. Garcia dressed in all black used a metal detector wand to scan bodies and check bags. Then, the smiling Leadership girl collected the ticket and wished everyone a wonderfully safe night.

Ms. Sexton monitored each tier but mainly helped the security guard with confiscating the banned collection of flasks, vape-pens, lighters, and anything else that would violate the conduct agreement. All three adults laughed at my peers' attempts to enjoy the poisons of this world. The adults wanted awareness of our demons. We wanted immunity to their consultations.

"Do you remember the scene from *House Party* when Bilal was singing this song?" Taniesha asked me and then began to sing, "*Alwwaays and foreveerr.*"

"Baby-babe, don't, please," I said and shook my head. "Leave it to the professionals."

"Take time to tell me, you really care," Taniesha sang and pretended her fist was a microphone. *"And we'll share tomorrow toooo-gether!"*

"Oh baby, stop, my ears," I begged while laughing, and then she laughed.

"I'll always love you forever," she whispered.

As the song played, our waltz came alive, increasing speed. Within seconds, the old school tune inspired more and more brave couples to gravitate toward the heart of the room. Across the bank hall, I noticed Trevon and Maria had returned to our reserved table. My best friend would be the first one to dance to an oldie record. Now he and Maria sat idle with their chairs facing one another like cranky parents ready to leave a party.

Trevon's arm rested on Maria's shoulder. She tried shrugging him off. He didn't budge. She pushed him away. He pointed to a red cup and then his pockets. She jumped out her seat and walked off toward the other side of the room. Trevon gave a sigh and hid his cup under the table. His finger stirred it for several seconds. He lifted his cocktail, took a long gulp, and then slammed the near empty cup on the table. His eyes stared coldly in my direction.

"What's happening at our table?" I asked Taniesha.

She gave that disarming smile again and squeezed my hand.

"Don't worry, be happy," she said. "Now hold me close. I want to feel you."

I held her hands and pulled her body near my chest. Her smooth arms tied around my back. Her gentle head rested on my shoulder. Her warm lips pressed on my neck. In mid-kiss, she looked at my face. Her brown eyes taught me the universe. Her soft touch rewarded me with everything else.

"Hmm, *piloerection*," Taniesha said and giggled. "No, it's nothing nasty. It literally means 'hair-raising' like goosebumps. I think you got piloerection on your neck for two reasons: Your skin is bunched up to hold in the temperature because you're cold. *Burrr.* But you don't feel cold. Yeah, it must be the second reason, overwhelming emotion like fear, awe, or *arousal*. So, which one are you feeling?"

"I think you already know," I said and winked. "But where did you learn all that stuff?"

"Remember Mr. Camus's Bio class?"

"How could I forget? That was the first time you, me, and Trevon all met."

"You *do* remember," she said with joy. "In fall semester I did my research project on goosebumps. Did you know that when creatures feel fear, their adrenaline kicks in and their hair stands on end? It comes from a fight-or-flight response like a defense mechanism for creatures against bigger threats, like porcupines versus bobcats. I guess, at the time, I thought the whole psychology of it was cool. You know I want to be a therapist. Hey, don't look at me like I'm crazy. Dude, I got an A+ on that assignment."

"I remember we all shared the same class together. When I first saw you with that tapered haircut and little sundress, you looked like Nia Long from *Friday*."

"You know, she ain't got nothing on me, and don't lose your steps," she said with a neck snap. Her right finger pointed at my feet that were offbeat to hers. "I remember you were so shy when we first met. You needed Trevon's help to talk to me. Do you remember when we were in the lab and Tre came over to my station? He had this corny-ass smile and was trying to walk like a pimp. Then he was like, 'Haaaavvve you met my friend, Jonah?' and just walked off, leaving you standing behind, hella awkward. And you remember what happened next?"

"Come on, really? Are we going to do this right now?"

"Don't act like you don't remember. Say what you said back then."

"Alright, alright, just for you. Hey babycakes."

She stomped her heel. "You didn't say that. Say it like how you said it, back then."

"Okay, chillax."

I stretched my neck, cleared my throat, and then took a deep breath.

"So, if I took your sweet face, put it on a pan, baked it in the oven for like thirty minutes, and then took it out to let it cool, you know what you'd be?"

"Hmmm, I don't know," she said in a tiny voice.

"You don't want to take a guess?"

"No."

"Okay, well, you would be a sweetie-pie."

"You said cutie-pie last time."

"Cutie, sweetie, same difference, same fucking pie."

"No, they're not. They're just different, okay?"

"Okay, whatever."

"Don't you *whatever* me. You're not getting special treatment. I don't care if there ain't no cure for the common birthday."

"Why did you just say that?"

DJ Amen scratched the record several times, making the beat pulsate with each rip. The music transitioned into Mac Dre's song, "Feeling myself." A mass of formally dressed teens swarmed to the center of the room as though the dreadlock Jesus himself was rapping through the huge speakers. Taniesha and I stepped aside and watched our peers morph into a mosh-pit, sparing no apologies to bumped shoulders and stomped feet. Ms. Sexton and Mr. Garcia were already on their way to tame the wild youth.

"I wish he'd play some Keyshia Cole," Taniesha said. "I ain't really feeling myself right here. Do you want to go somewhere else, like upstairs? Trevon told me about the upper floor being empty, maybe if, you know."

"I love you," I nodded and kissed her above the nose. "Like I really *really* love you."

Taniesha gazed into my eyes and casted a spell of desire upon my lips. Before my mouth parted again, a thought had occurred. The first time I admitted those three words, I was in between her legs about to make love to her body.

"Do you really mean it?" she asked and leaned back surprised.

"Yes, I love you more than music, books, movies, my phone, school, my family, my 'so-called' friends. Sheesh, I wish I didn't love you so much. Do you believe me?"

She looked at the couple next to us. Their lips locked together, oblivious to the world. Taniesha's eyes sparkled with delight, but within moments, her frown removed all joy.

"Yes, but my mama would disagree." She paused and searched for the right words. "She always told me that a man who makes his love known only by words is a fool."

"Not true. If you lost me, you'd know I loved you, and I'd go on loving you."

"You sound like a movie. I don't want to lose you, so why say that?"

"I don't know. I got a lot on my mind. Let's talk about something else."

"No, I don't understand you. Why can't you just talk to me?"

"I am talking to you," I said and raised my voice.

Taniesha studied my discontent. Her only reaction was to nod. She rested her head along my chest. We held each other, slowly rocking from side to side to our own tune. My eyes drifted off toward Ms. Sexton who was dispersing students in spite of the Mac Dre song not being over. She laughed at their jeers and boos and continued redirecting the thick crowd.

"Let's keep this fun kiddos," Ms. Sexton said and turned her back to their middle fingers.

Once the dance floor cleared up a bit, I noticed Raynold and Sasha standing near the wall away from everyone. They both had red cups in their hands. Maria appeared from the thinning crowd. She approached Sasha and both girls hugged for more than a minute. Raynold shook his head and switched his cup with Sasha's during the embrace. Sasha offered the cup to Maria seemingly unaware. She gulped down Raynold's mixed concoction as if the drink was water.

"We really need to talk," Taniesha said and rubbed my cheek.

"Here we go again." I rolled my eyes. "Why do you always want to talk?"

"Nah, don't do that. You're the one acting hella moody like in the car. I hope it wasn't the molly-talk. Me and Maria weren't going to take any, I swear. No, that's not it. Is it because we have four more weeks left of school? I feel like you've been acting weird because of the long distance thing. Are you afraid you might lose me if I move out to the east coast? I'm sorry to bring it up again, but just tell me this. Are you scared of the future? It's okay. I am too."

"What if I said, I didn't want to go?"

"Go where?" she asked and looked around. "Home? College? What do you mean?"

I pointed to a far away place. "What if we just ran away somewhere? Like you and I could drive and leave California, maybe the whole country. We can travel somewhere small like a rural town near Canada. Then we'll get our passports and travel around the world like to Africa. We'll see Egypt and the pyramids. What do you think about that?"

Taniesha pulled my hand to her side. I gripped her waist.

"Africa's far," she said and laughed. "But what about Europe? We can see Greece, Spain, maybe France and see the Eiffel Tower, and then visit Amsterdam and smoke our lungs black."

"Really?"

"Are you *really* talking about doing that now? I can't abandon everyone I know. I'm not going to drop out of college and roam around the world like some international hobo. Maybe later, when I'm older, but I'm seventeen, and you're barely legal too. Next thing you'll do is ask to get married."

"You think I want us to turn out like my parents? No, I'm not crazy. I want to be free. No, I want to be free with you. We can be free together. Can't you see we only have now? Tomorrow isn't promised, so listen, if we ran away, everything would be better."

"Life is already good. Why would you want to run away?"

"Because it all feels so pointless. Everything. Don't you see?"

The longer I held her waist, the more I grew aware she would never understand how I felt. I removed my hand from her hip. We both took a deep breath, but our moment had fled.

"Just calm down and breathe," she instructed. "*Woosah. Woo-sah.*"

"Are you not going with me? Otherwise, I don't see the point."

"I guess I don't get it," she said and gave a fake laugh. "Let's just dance, okay?"

"I don't want to waltz anymore. Just tell me, is it yes or no?"

"No Jonah, I ain't making that decision right now. Let's talk later."

I stopped waltzing. Taniesha remained, rocking from side to side. Our bodies detached.

"You're not taking me seriously, so how about this? Let's not talk at all."

"Finally."

When she reached for my cheek, I brushed away her hand like a pestering fly.

"Stop."

"You're acting hella immature," she said. "What's your problem?"

"You have the problem."

"If you're going to act like this, why are you even with me?"

"I don't know."

Taniesha's hands rubbed her wet eyes, trying to wipe away her running mascara like she did in the car. But this time was more serious. Her chest started to pant and heave.

"Why, after everything we've been through, why?" she cried. "No, there ain't no way for me to love you if you won't let me. No, fuck you, Jonah. I don't deserve this. I'm going to have fun, and be happy without you. You don't love me. Ain't no way you do."

"Taniesha, I'm sorry. Don't cry. I don't know what I'm saying. I'm so sorry."

"No Jonah. You can't say that. Every sorry after the first apology doesn't mean shit."

"Kiss me. I love you."

When I reached for her hand, she smacked my wrist.

"Let go. I hate you," she said.

"Wait, let's just talk."

"It's too late. I'm gone."

Taniesha marched off, bumping the waltzing couple in her path. She walked across the room to our reserved table where Trevon sat alone. She leaned into his shoulder and took his hand. Taniesha and Trevon took turns speaking into each other's ears. Her face broke into a waterfall of tears. Trevon stood up, touched her cheeks, pulled her close. They embraced.

Piloerection.

The strobe lights danced around the bank hall. Twinkles of absolution spread within a room of darkness. The large Flava-Flav clock on the entrance wall revealed the midnight hour close at hand. Soon I would turn eighteen, an adult in the world's view. Age was simply a number to a broken child against pervading time.

"And I tremble lest the darkness teach me that nothing matters."

Seconds or minutes passed by as I stood stunned on the dance floor like a Black mannequin. My eyes were open, blind to the change taking place. Trevon and Taniesha were absent from the table, somewhere unknown, probably together.

I gripped my bracelet tight. My fingers traced the lettering. No matter how much I tried to hold on, she was already gone.

"Wake up, Jonah, you seen Taniesha?" Sasha asked, creeping up from behind. "I hella need to talk to her. It's an emergency."

"No," I replied and noticed her red cup was full. "Is that what I think it is?"

"For real, it's serious," she said and looked at our reserve table. "It's Maria, Jonah."

"May I?"

I grabbed the cup from her hand. My mouth gulped down the entire concoction. My body shivered from the warm bitter taste.

"Thanks," I said.

"Holy shit," she said, her mouth gasping in shock. "You know what you just did?"

"I don't give a fuck."

My feet departed from the dance floor, passing by Sasha, Raynold, and all the remaining players on stage. I made my way to an unguarded entrance. My exit. Outside the bank hall, the sky was black. The cold air sent goosebumps down my neck and spine. Boxy cars roared and honked through Sansome Street. Loud strangers followed the sidewalk maze of San Francisco.

Every piece of shit around me had erupted into a philharmonic orchestra of sounds, but nothing really mattered.

My loneliness made the loudest noise.

CHAPTER 6
TiMeLess

F riden 11:19 p.m.

"A fight for love and glory, a case of do or die, as time goes by!"

Behind the Old Federal Reserve building, a woman sang off key followed by a male voice who ad-libbed out of tune. A clutter of steps tapped closer and closer to the staircase. From the pathway appeared a gray-haired white lady in a red dress and a bald white man in a black suit. I sat up from the staircase, leaned against the Monument of Analysis statue, and pretended to act cool. Upon seeing me alone, the white folks froze mid-stride like two distracted squirrels.

"Oh, howdie, we're sorry," the woman said. Her arm dropped to her side, holding an unlit cigarette. "No one's allowed back here. You're supposed to be inside with the rest of the kiddos."

A chirp rang from the man's pocket. He brought the walkie-talkie close to his mouth.

"Everybody's *jumping*? Repeat that, over," he said and listened to the muffled voice. He patted the woman's shoulder. "I'm going back inside. We'll pick this up later. Take five."

"Alright Dave," the woman said and waved at his back. Once the man disappeared, she searched her Burberry purse and pulled out a red lighter. *Click. Flick. Click.* The flame ignited the white tip. She brought the lit cigarette to her thin lips.

"You mind?" she asked and took a puff. "Do you like the *Time-Goes-By* theme of prom? Be honest."

"Honestly, the theme is stupid," I said and stared at the ground. "Why does everything need a theme? Why does everything need a message or point to it? If that was the case then you wouldn't be smoking those cancer sticks."

"Oh, I know, I know," she admitted and took another puff. "You're so right."

"I guess, we would rather be the moth than the flame."

The woman exhaled a mass of smoke. Within the cloud, I saw a fleeing ghost, disappearing into the moonlight.

"Keon?" I called.

"What'd you say?" the woman asked and flicked the cigarette ashes. The wind carried the debris onto the statue. "You know, it was so funny when we walked up. I was singing Sam's piano tune, 'As Time Goes By,' well, trying too at least. I'm not a very good singer, can you tell? When I found out the prom's theme was like the title of the song, I was laughing to myself because I knew you lil' kiddos wouldn't know a single thing about Casablanca or Ilsa and Rick. You don't have a clue what I'm talking about, now do you?"

"Yeah, I know that movie, but didn't Ilsa and them call the Black piano player, *boy*?"

"Well, you know," she said and lowered her cigarette. "Those were the times back then. You know things were different. Not like now. Now where's your pretty date?"

I pointed toward the prom entrance. "I don't know, somewhere inside."

"I bet she's a nail-biter," she said and winked.

"I don't know what that means."

"How long have you been out here?"

When I glanced at my phone, the screen said nine messages, eleven missed calls.

"I don't know. An hour, I guess."

"What have you been doing the whole time?" she asked.

"By the way, our theme is timeless, not the one you were talking about from *Casablanca*. Timeless is something different."

"Interesting. Well, they sound the same, but I think you ignored my question."

"No, they're not the same."

"Watch your tone, young man," she said while wagging her finger.

"What does timeless even mean when nothing can be timeless, except time? Time waits for no one. Time is forever. Time knows when one's fate ends and another begins. Time will always be, even when there is no life."

"Oki doki." She paused and puffed heavily on her cigarette. "So, what are you like, Mr. Philosopher or something?"

"No, I'm Mr. Jonah, and I don't know much. It's just that I *had* a friend. He was a really *good* friend like an older brother. He gave me a bunch of books. Last thing he told me before he died was to memorize them like they did in that one novel, Fair, Fahren, I forgot the title. Shit, I think I'm losing it."

"Don't curse."

The woman flicked the cigarette butt onto the ground and stomped it with her heel. When I stood up, my phone slipped out onto the concrete steps. She watched me, anticipating my next move. I didn't reach for the phone. Nothing appeared broken.

"I'm going to turn eighteen at midnight. I don't feel old though."

"There's still no cure for the common birthday," she said. "Shoot, I remember when I was eighteen and my first prom." She gazed up at the dark sky and spoke toward the night. "Hmm, what can I say? I guess, you're only as old as you feel. Tonight's the youngest you'll ever be again. That's the best advice I can give you."

"But a good scare is better than good advice."

"Alright, young man. You win. I'm going back inside. I suggest you do the same."

The woman let out a sigh and caressed my shoulder. I flinched. She frowned and walked away the same path she came. My body was left alone with the ashes and scent of her history.

"There's a serious side in everything I say," a blonde woman rapped on the corner of Sansome Street. *"Life is too short for you to wait 'til the next day..."*

I sat by myself on the steps behind the Old Federal Reserve. My eyes watched the small woman recite Too Short's lyrics to an empty corner. She stood next to a green bicycle but had no helmet on. Her blue floral dress was two sizes too big, yet the gown couldn't hide her watermelon belly. She rubbed her swollen stomach, climbed onto the bike, and then pedaled across a two-way street during a red light. A passing car nearly clipped her back tire.

Honk. Shout. Honk. Shout.

The pregnant woman didn't care. She wanted her baby to die. Some people would cry if the woman got run over or killed. Regardless of her death, the earth would continue spinning and spinning until the sun exploded. The universe would give birth to new planets and solar systems. The cycle of life would keep rotating like it always had. No one would ever know why, only that life wasn't worth living. Maybe the blonde woman knew the universal truth: To put much value into anything was absolutely absurd.

"In my category I'm the one and only," the blonde woman continued rapping and rode off into the distance. *"And I'm a stay short but funky..."*

At that moment, I understood what I needed to do: Opposite action prescribed by Dr. Imani. I would march into the bank hall, find Taniesha sitting at the table, give her a thousand kisses, and sweep her off her feet like that one scene from that one movie. A spotlight would illuminate our walk onto the dance floor. The crowd would clap and cheer. My girlfriend would smile and say: "I love you."

Boyz II Men would start singing "End of the Road" in the background.

I would hold my girlfriend's hand, and admit I knew the relationship would end before it started, for I was the fool who wanted to ride this rollercoaster anyway. The music would grow silent in suspense. Taniesha would smile again and sing falsetto: *"Love conquers all thiiinnngs!"*

The room would erupt in applause. Moments would pass with the weighing grievances. Time would teach more than all mistakes. Any absurdity would vanish from our uncertainties.

"Although we've come to the end of the road, still I can't let go..."

My mind snapped out of the daze, humming Boyz II Men. When I stood up quickly, pins-and-needles struck my legs. I had sat too long on the steps, yet I couldn't recall the past hour. Everything felt foggy, but I marched on toward my reconciliation. My feet tiptoed around the Monument of Analysis statue and limped down the back pathway. I entered the lobby doors in search of my love.

"I need you, Taniesha."

Once inside the building, I walked past the Leadership girl who sat near the booth hypnotized by her phone. Mr. Garcia, Mr. Haley, Ms. Sexton, and the other chaperones were nowhere around the main entrance. Everyone seemed situated at the heart of the bank hall.

"I'm sorry, Taniesha."

The dark room glowed with bright red colors. Strobe light beams painted the walls with blurry rainbows. My nose was overcome by body-spray and booty sweat from twerking couples. Above the dance floor, D.J Amen stood over the people, maneuvering the buttons on his radiant laptop. The music shaman led his followers in a séance. The players shed their masks and robes, surrendering to their inhibitions.

"Forgive me, Taniesha."

At the center of the room was the tall lanky white boy in an ugly suit. He chewed on a plastic straw along with his date who was sweating through her white dress.

He walked over to a Black couple, shook both their hands, and departed as they put straws in their mouths. The white boy returned to his date and wiped her wet forehead with his jacket sleeve. Then he stared in my direction, shaking his head.

"I love you, Taniesha."

My body passed through the crowd of groping hands and grinding hips. I arrived at the reserved table, only to find remnants of my friends' visit. Empty red cups. Two chairs slanted against the table. The white satin tablecloth dragged to the floor as if tugged on from inside.

"Who's there?" I asked and lifted up the cloth.

Maria was cowered next to the table leg. I reached for her sweaty hand and slowly pulled her out from under the table.

"What are you doing?"

"What's going on? What's happening?" she mumbled and released my hand.

Maria stood up and wobbled from side to side, eventually falling back into her chair. Once firmly seated, she rocked back and forth, kicking her legs in spasms.

"Why were you on the floor?"

"I don't need your help Tre," she said and studied my face. Black streaks of make-up ran down her cheeks. "Get the fuck off me."

"It's me Maria. Jonah."

"Who's Maria-Jonah?" She pulled on her hair. "No, why are you fucking with my head? Why's it so hot right now? I think I feel like I'm going to explode."

"You gotta relax. I think you're hella on one. You have to tell me where's Taniesha and Trevon. Where's everyone?"

"Just stop, stop it, please." Her voice grew tense. "Stop it, stop spinning."

I reached for her shoulder. She swatted my hand.

"You have to control yourself. You're going to draw too much attention."

Maria rattled her head and shouted, "No means no means no!"

"Whoa, what's wrong with you?"

I reached again for her open hand. She roared like a lioness, calling the attention of nearby eyes and ears.

"Wait, I'm not the bad guy. I just want to help."

"No, I said no!" she shouted again and pounded her fist on the table. "No, don't you ever touch me again. No, Tre, I told you I don't want to."

Maria paused then her body jerked in short spasms. Her chest heaved with each heavy breath. Her frantic arms wailed around as if possessed by a demon.

"What's going on? You got the bubble-guts?"

"No, why are you doing this to me?" she pleaded. "I think I'm pregnant."

"Ah man, I ain't got time for that."

From the dance floor stood a Black couple watching with their mouths dropped. The guy tapped the person next to him, pointed at us, and watched. A row of people formed near our table, talking into each other's ears, playing telephone, and watching us. Ms. Sexton broke through the still crowd and marched toward our table.

"Sit up, I said sit up," I ordered her. "The A.P's coming."

Slowly, Maria obeyed.

"Hello Mr. Tarver," Ms. Sexton said. "Is there a problem over here?"

"No, no problem, ma'am," I said.

"I hope not. We've had this talk before. What's with your friend?"

Maria bobbed her head up and down. She mumbled with her lips closed.

Ms. Sexton turned to her. "Excuse me, what's your name, hun?"

"She's talking to you," I told Maria.

My hands rubbed her shoulder. Her body was unresponsive. I turned to Ms. Sexton.

"It's her head, I think her head hurts. She might be sick. Her date is here. He'll be back. He's in his car. She's okay. I'm fine. How are you?"

"If she's not feeling well, we better call home," Ms. Sexton said and leaned into Maria. "How are you feeling, sweetie?"

"What the fuck?" she replied.

Maria's face dripped with sweat. Her lungs panted heavily. Her mouth gasped.

"Oh my God!"

Maria's torso twisted to the side of her chair. I took a step back. She hugged her stomach as a crowd surrounded the show. I took two steps back. Her head hung low with bloated cheeks ready to burst. Once beyond arm's reach, I watched an outpour of dark liquids and solids erupt from Maria's mouth. Ms. Sexton and I jumped back, barely missing splashes of vomit.

"Jesus Christ, no, both of you, stay here," Ms. Sexton ordered and picked up her walkie-talkie. "Come in, staff. Need help in the back. We got another incident. Sexton, over."

While the Assistant Principal was preoccupied with the growing crowd and red orange puke, I retreated from the table toward the bathroom. Mr. Garcia broke through the huddled bodies and surveyed the scene. I ducked behind the bathroom doorway. The A.P and the security guard carefully lifted Maria's comatose body from her seat. Both adults waved at the crowd to clear some space. I looked around the large room, searching for someone familiar.

"First Sasha's ass, now Maria," a slurred voice spoke from behind the bathroom door.

I pulled the doorknob and discovered Raynold bobbing his head. His eyes were bloodshot red. He gave me a fist bump and then pointed toward the entrance.

"Said the night wind to the little lamb," Raynold sang to an unheard melody.

"What happened to Maria?" I asked. "Where's everyone? What did you see?"

"Do you see what I see? Way up in the sky, little lamb."

"Stop playing around and tell me what's going on? What happened to Taniesha and Tre?"

Raynold erupted in laughter and then continued singing to himself.

"Do you see what I see? A star, a star, dancing in the night with a tail as big as a kite."

I slapped his face hard. Drool fell from his lips.

"What the fuck! You didn't have to slap me bruh," he said and rubbed his cheek. "Why you trying to fuck up my high?"

"You can't be singing Christmas carols right now," I released my grip on his shirt. "Look around. Shit's falling apart. The police will probably be here soon."

"Ain't no 5-0 catching my Black ass," he replied, massaging his face with both hands. "They take Tre and them before me because they hella gone. I mean, I took one with him. She bitched out. She took half a one. And she took the whole one."

"Wait, what? You're not making sense." I shook my head and tried not to imagine my best friend and girlfriend together. "No, Taniesha told me she wouldn't do it. Where are they?"

"On the stairway to heaven," he said and pointed at a staircase leading to the upper floor.

"How long have they been up there?"

"Oh, fucking." He paused and then licked his lips. "Fucking forever, I think. Wait, how does the rest of that song go? *'Do you hear what I hear?'* Come on, join me, and sing."

"There's no time."

I ignored Raynold and ran to the stairway. I wasn't sure when or how, but my emotions began to cloud my conscience and possess my every movement. My feet climbed each step by step up the staircase. My body ducked under the yellow tape covering the open entrance.

No one was around.

The upper floor was empty and quiet, except for the music echoing downstairs. The dark corridor had a few set tables and chairs, plus a restroom in the far back. My legs continued marching inside, walking farther away from the sounds of prom. A faint moan became clearer the closer my ears approached the restroom. Piloerection crept on my neck. My ears reached the door, hearing two voices, not one.

"I wanted to be a good man, though I pinched my soul."

Slowly, my hand pulled back the handle. Inside the bathroom were gray walls and a white sink. Bent over the faucet was Taniesha's brown body. Her blue dress was lifted high above her waist. Trevon stood behind her. His black slacks were wrapped around his ankles. Her butt clapped from his thrusting pelvis. Her hips jiggled from each pump. He turned his sweaty face in my direction.

"Oh fuck, oh fuck," Trevon yelled. "I think I'm close, oh, oh my God!"

My arms rushed at them both, pushing Trevon first to the bathroom floor and then Taniesha against the sink. My knees pressed onto Trevon's chest, pinning him to the ground. He tried pulling up his underwear and pants. My fists punched his chin and jaw.

"Oh my God!" Taniesha screamed. "Jonah, stop it, stop it."

Trevon reached for Taniesha's aid. My hands grabbed his shirt. My fists smashed everything on his face.

"Stop it, you're going to kill him," she said. "Please stop, please Jonah."

My right arm swung back. Taniesha pulled on my shoulder. My arm escaped from her clutch. My elbow struck her stomach. She fell to the tile floor and crawled on all fours. My hands released Trevon's collar. My weight pounced on Taniesha lying on her back.

"Why would you act like you cared? No, I thought you loved me."

Her eyes cried. My teeth clenched. We both sighed.

"Why would you fuck up everything? No, this is your fault, Taniesha."

My voice cracked. Her jaw trembled. We both gasped.

"No Jonah, please don't," she pleaded. "No, please don't do this."

Taniesha held onto my wrists. Her nails dug into my arm. My body jolted back from the sting. My eyes closed. My mouth hollered. My fist punched her with all my strength. My eyes opened. My girlfriend lay on the tile floor, curled up, motionless.

My lips read, "You did this."

My bloody hands turned on the faucet and lathered up with a ton of soap. My red fingers danced under the running water. My bruised hands dried off with a paper towel and then wiped the smeared blood off my tuxedo.

My heavy feet walked toward the bathroom door, stepping over Trevon who was squirming toward the corner stall. His black pants were still wrapped around his ankles. With each desperate crawl, he left a greasy river of blood along his path. Trevon coughed up dark liquid and mumbled some words that would never make a difference. I didn't give a fuck about anyone anymore. Nothing mattered.

Time destroyed all things.

CHAPTER 7
PARADISE

S aturday 12:02 a.m.

Drip. Drip. Drip.

I might've killed my best friend and girlfriend on my eighteenth birthday. My body sat in the Mercedes driver's seat, still shaken from my recent actions. I watched blood drip from my bloody knuckles onto the steering wheel. Trevon used to tease me and say, "Your hands look like baseball mitts made of Snickers."

No more stupid jokes.

I sat alone, staring at the blood drip, drip onto the keys hung in the ignition slot. Taniesha used to warn me and say, "You keep leaving your keys in, you'll drain the battery."

No more annoying advice.

I sat in silence, gazing at the blood drip, drip, drip onto my black slacks. My mama used to advise me and say, "There ain't a spot that bleach can't fix."

No more normalcy.

I was in blood, stepped in so far that I could not wade a return to the past. I felt like a boy, still. The midnight hour defined me as a man. In the rearview mirror reflected a criminal.

Drip.

Outside my car window, I noticed Ms. Sexton approaching the staircase behind the Old Federal Reserve. The Assistant Principal stood next to the Monument of Analysis statue. Soon, she was joined by the cigarette woman whom I had spoken to earlier. They walked in separate directions, in search of the bad guy with blood on his hands. My body sat upright, only high enough for my eyes to see them not see me.

Drip. Drip.

Someone must have found Taniesha and Trevon in the bathroom, barely breathing. Someone probably called the ambulance and police. Soon the E.M.Ts would arrive and check if my girlfriend and best friend were dead. Someone would snitch and target "Jonah Tarver" as their main suspect.

Drip. Drip. Drip

Somehow the police will find my location. They will ask me several questions about the drugs and alcohol, and then place me under arrest. Somewhere I will make a call home in the middle of the night to hear my mama pick up the phone, already knowing something was wrong, only to say, "Everything will be okay baby, I wish I could take all of your problems away." Somehow my father will take the phone and say, "Guilty before proven innocent," a phrase he'd claimed about Black men, but never his own. In the end, I will atone for my bloody sins.

"Over there!"

The cigarette woman shouted and pointed at the Mercedes. Ms. Sexton spoke into her walkie-talkie. My body cowered into the driver's seat, hoping they wouldn't recognize me from afar. I grabbed a dry rag, ripped the cloth in half, and wrapped it around my bloody hands. Both women were racing down the steps, pointing in my direction, yelling words I couldn't understand. They must've followed my blood trail. If I stayed parked any longer, they'd catch me. My world as I knew it was extinct. Time opened a new path.

Drive.

I turned the keys, revved the engine. The Mercedes sped off. Tires skirted, swerving in and out of the white lanes, pushing thirty, forty, fifty miles per hour. One street onto the next. One corner after another. One block, two blocks, four blocks, one widening vortex of loss.

I'm lost.

Where am I going?

I didn't know where I was going as my mind saw flashes of a bloody bathroom, bloody faces, and bloody hands. Somehow my body went into auto-pilot, commanding the wheel and pedals as the car kept speeding, speeding away toward no home. No, home would've been the first place the police would look. No, home was where the hatred lived. I needed to find my safe place, or as Dr. Imani called it, "the safe space," so I had to keep speeding away from this loss.

What am I doing?

I didn't know what I was doing as though my mind was spiraling out of control like my body grew numb, or was it the other way around? The car continued racing, racing without a destination, racing down south, or was it north? I should check my G.P.S, my phone. No, I didn't want to see my notifications. No, I needed to keep racing along the coast. Yes, just race across the border with only my driver's license and birthday money. Yes, keep racing and escaping, and speeding with faith in a fateful purpose to a pointless world that has one absurd truth: Life has no point, only loss.

Who am I?

I didn't know who I was anymore, except a lost body running for an escape. I was my thirteen-year-old self after learning about Keon's death. "It was no one's fault," my father had said. I wondered if he would say the same words today after learning of my mistakes. No, I wasn't lost, just running toward a new future, a new hope without Taniesha or Trevon. No, she was responsible for this bullshit. Why was her blue dress so bloody? No, he ruined everything. Why was his face so bloody? I should've never gone to prom with them. Why were my hands so bloody? No, I should've never gone to prom at all.

"You did this."

My mind floated everywhere. My heart fought against every imagined idea. No, I didn't want to kill myself or harm anyone else. This worry needed to die, the one boiling inside like a looming nervous breakdown. This fear needed to surrender and submit before my core erupted. But worry and fear were ideas that could never die, only kill their host. When the mind has received an idea, the body will ingest every fate and possibility, affecting all desires and actions. With time, the idea will grow and fester like a spreading cancer within the host's former self. In time, the host will no longer seem recognizable, yet the idea will remain like a shadow. Not long ago, my worries and fears taught me that nothing mattered. Within the darkness, I was never fully living, but rather just killing time.

Stop.

Red light.

"Where am I? How long have I been driving?" I asked myself.

My mind snapped out of another daze. My foot slammed on the brakes. My hands steadied the wheel. My eyes looked around to try and recognize the San Francisco street signs. No cars were nearby. No one in sight, except a tall Black female in a hot pink mini-skirt, strolling the sidewalk. She stopped near my car and flashed her stuffed black bra. Her large hands waved in my direction. I rolled down the window, and at closer look, her brown chiseled face appeared covered in dark make-up. She had straight hips, shapely calves, and stocky feet like a bodybuilder on a midnight walk, I assumed. My father would likely judge otherwise.

"What's cooking, good-looking?" she said in a deep high pitched voice. "I'm Peaches. What you doing? Where you headed?"

My hands trembled on the steering wheel. My feet rumbled along the brakes.

"Funny you should ask," I said. "Honestly, I don't know where I'm going, what I'm doing, or who I am. I feel so alone. I think I need help."

"Got-damn, what happened to your hands?" she asked and laughed like an evil villain.

"It was, no, I was in an accident."

"Relax now, *woosah*." She took a deep breath. "I'm Peaches. What you looking to do?"

"I think, I just need to know which way is Mexico."

"Why eat tacos when you can taste *Peaches*?"

"Wait, what? Taste what?"

"Peaches, come on. I said my name three times already like Beetlejuice."

She paused and leaned closer to my window. Her body smelled of alcohol and regrets.

"Hold up, how old are you anyways?" she asked.

"I'm eighteen, but I don't feel like it. I think I'm horny, but I don't think I love myself."

Green light.

"I don't think you ready for this jelly," she said.

Peaches shifted glances at my attire, the traffic light, and then the Mercedes. Her hands clapped twice. A white smile appeared amidst two red lips.

"Know what?" she said. "I think you'll find what you want on Market street. This place called the Garden of Eden got what you need. They're definitely more up your alley."

"What? Where?"

"Garden of Eden. You can't miss paradise." She pointed behind me. "Watch out."

A pair of high-beams flashed. The car honked then revved its engine.

"Which direction?"

Peaches pulled the end of her skirt, covering her knees, and then retreated to the corner.

"See you later."

With nowhere else really to go, I decided paradise was my destination. My feet released the brakes and pressed the gas. I turned the Mercedes left and down onto Market street, cruising through one traffic light after the next. To my left and right were the living dead roaming during dark hours. Party-goers rotated between exiting and entering the clubs. Drunks crowded outside the bars. Substance abusers and peddlers solicited near the liquor stores. Each block displayed the same business and same stranger, except different names. Perhaps I was already dead like the rest of them. Maybe San Francisco was my purgatory. My shadow was possibly death following at every turn, tipping my hand toward my final destination, or was it my angel?

Outside my window, I saw a large neon banner that read: GARDEN OF EDEN. Below the glowing sign was a green silhouette of a woman with curves like Jessica Rabbit. Her hand held a red apple. Her leg was wrapped around a loose tree branch.

You can't miss paradise.

I pulled the car over to the side, across the street from the entrance. Four Asian men in business suits were at the front, smoking cigarettes. The men were short and old, probably Chinese, in their forties, but one could never tell the true age of Asian people.

The main door opened, startling the group. A bald muscular man appeared in a tight shiny black shirt, size extra-medium. He walked up to the four men, stood with his arms crossed, and barked a few words. The men tossed out their cigarettes and retreated through the door. The bald man walked over to the area with an air freshener, covered his face, and sprayed wildly for several seconds. He looked in my direction, shook his head, and then returned inside.

"What if the only paradise was a paradise lost?"

My foot pressed the gas and sped off. My eyes searched left and right for a place to park. Finding an empty space in San Francisco had become a hell all on its own. Every street was a rat maze arranged with an endless row of parked cars. Each sidewalk was flooded with posting after posting of a time limit sign, a disability sign, a construction site sign, but no "Hey you park here" sign. Even the pay-to-park lots were either full or closed.

After circulating the car around back toward Market street, I finally found an open compact space and drove straight in. I peeked out my window, noticing the broken meter. Above was a street sign covered in graffiti and party stickers. I might have parked at the worst spot in the neighborhood in spite of having no other choice. In the distance awaited paradise, perhaps my purpose.

"What if the path to paradise was the beginning of hell?"

I rewrapped the wet rag on my hands, but my bruises looked worse than a bare-knuckle boxer. My body stepped out of the car, secured all the doors tightly, and then beeped the alarm lock twice. My feet marched toward my destination, only guided by my recent recollection. Each fleeting step brought a cringe to my neck, a slight glance behind my shoulder, an unnerving suspicion of my shadow. In the nearby darkness leered death, or perhaps someone else.

"Keon?"

What if my best friend was really an angel watching from above, guiding my hands and feet toward safety, in spite of myself? Keon never told me why I needed to memorize the Langston Hughes poem. He had only said the lines saved him, and that one day it will save me.

"But now I lie beneath cool loam, forgetting every dream, and in this narrow bed of earth, no lights gleam."

Right before my eyes appeared the large neon banner and female silhouette. Straight ahead flashed the words: GARDEN OF EDEN. The front was empty, awaiting my arrival. The main door stood between walls cluttered with artwork of a flaming sword. A heavy bass thumped from inside the entrance. Nowhere outside appeared any postings or words about a strip club.

"Please don't judge me," I uttered to the wind.

The door swung open. Two middle-aged white men dressed in collared shirts and khakis stepped out the entrance. Both were laughing to themselves. They ignored the Black boy in a tuxedo standing near the doorway. They walked side by side toward the corner and pulled out their cigarette packs.

"Dude, can you believe that chick did us both?" the man with a crew cut said. "What was her name anyway?"

"She told us like two different ones," his tanned friend said and then glanced in my direction. "Hey, let the big homie pass."

"My bad, brother," the crew-cut man apologized and propped open the door. "Good luck and good fuck."

"What does that mean? What's it like in there?"

Both men traded glances at each other, holding in their laughter. The crew-cut man tapped his friend's shoulder and then leaned into my ear.

"I'll put it like this," he whispered. "Everything you can imagine is real."

I nodded knowingly then stepped inside. The door closed behind me. I entered a dimly lit purple lobby, receiving a warm whiff of perfumed booty sweat. Between a set of purple drapes stood a booth with vibrant head paintings of a sphinx, griffin, and lion. Above the booth was an admission price list and a purple stone plaque that read:

And the Lord God planted
A garden in Eden,
And there he put the man
Whom he had formed.

Within the booth was a short Latina wearing a low-cut pink shirt, clipped with a tag that read: MY NAME IS SONIA. Her bobbing head was plugged to earbuds. Her thick lashes and dark eyes watched me approach.

"This is the end, my only friend, the end," Sonia sang and then tapped her ear.

"Hello, my name is Jonah," I said, real formal as hell.

"The Doors just be putting me in another zone, for real," she said and nodded. "Have you ever felt that way, like being in another space, or another world?"

"I guess so," I replied, and then a shiver crawled down my spine. "But no."

"How do you know this is all real or just a dream?"

"I don't know."

"I'm just fucking with you," she said and giggled. "How can I help you, young sir?"

"Well, I couldn't help but notice your lovely purple establishment," I said and pointed at the plaque above her. "I was wondering what's with all the Bible stuff?"

"It's feng shui," she replied. "So what's with you? Were you at a wedding or something? Did you want to come inside or just admire the walls? Wait, you got I.D?"

"Yeah, I'm eighteen, is that okay?"

I pulled out my driver's license and tried showing it to Sonia, while at the same time covering my bruises.

"Oh wow, you're just a baby boy," she said, studying my card and face. "Nah, you're a pretty brave baby too. There's still ain't no cure for the common birthday."

"Who told you to say that?"

She pointed to the price sign above. "For you, it's twenty-five to get in."

Sonia handed back my I.D and dropped her smile. I gave her a hundred-dollar bill, the same one my mama slipped in the journal as my birthday gift. She used a counterfeit pen to check off the bill. She placed it inside the cash register then gathered several small bills from separate trays. Without haste, she counted the returned amount on the counter and then stacked the bills neatly on the counter. Somehow, I felt rich and poor at the same time.

"What would my mama think of me now?"

"What'd you say? Oh this, we do it with everybody." She paused and pointed to my forearm. "Let me see your wrist right quick."

"It's not what you think," I replied and lowered my bruised hands.

"Just say you ain't no Black Jeffrey Dahmer," she said and squinted her eyes.

I raised my hands for her inspection. "My bad, this was just an accident, really."

"Yo, you can't be bleeding in the club. For real, that shit ain't cute. The girls are going to think you up to something. They know if you're hella nervous."

"I'm not nervous. I'm cooler than the other side of the pillow."

"Is this your first time?" she asked, already knowing the answer.

"Are they nice to first timers?" I replied.

She gave a devilish grin and nodded. "This stamp gives you free in-and-outs. Show it to Wells behind the drapes to let you in. Lastly, *Abandon every hope, ye who enter here.*"

"Well, okay, that's kind of dark. Wait, is that a part of the feng shui?"

"Enjoy paradise, baby boy," she laughed and tapped her earbuds. *"This is the end, my only friend, the end..."*

Sonia retreated to her chair, singing to herself and texting on her phone. I waved bye and walked through the thick purple curtains. Within an instant, I was greeted by the same tanned muscular man from earlier outside whom I assumed was their bouncer.

"Let's make this quick James Bond," Wells said and pointed to my tuxedo. His deep voice and rugged accent sounded like an Italian version of Mr. T. "Just show me your wrist."

I extended my arm. Wells examined my wrist and bandages. I already knew what he was going to say next.

"What the hell happened to your hands?" he asked.

"You see, I got scratched up fixing a flat tire on the bridge, but I'm fine," I replied, real cool as hell. "It's healing nicely though. Thanks for asking. How are you? Having a fine night?"

"We don't allow no trouble here at the Garden of Eden." He squinted his bushy eyebrows. His large fists clenched at his side. "If you can't obey, you'll be kicked out of paradise."

"That's pretty on the nose," I said and stared on his badge. "Your name is Wells, as in Orson Welles? That's cool, but honestly, *Citizen Kane* is hella over-rated. Most folks like it, but they miss the point at the end."

"Listen buddy, if the dancers say sit, you sit."

"You mean strippers?"

"*Dancers*. Don't interrupt me. Like I was saying, if the dancers say jump, you jump. You understand? The ATM inside takes most cards, but there's a bunch of banks nearby. Bathrooms in the lobby. And we close at four. Questions?"

"Where should I sit?"

"First timer?"

"What if I say yes?"

Wells gave the same wide grin that Sonia had a minute ago. He stepped aside and pointed to the stage.

"Oh, they'll treat you real nice up front," he said.

"Thanks?"

I walked through the curtain gate into Eden, greeted by Prince's song, "Do me baby" playing from the corner speakers. I stood within the center aisle between the rows of movie theater seats. In the center of the room stood a large empty stage, a long silver pole, and a collage of reflective mirrors set in the background. Within the glass was my blurry image from afar watching myself. In the front chairs, a group of Asian men in business suits sat patiently, staring in my direction. Their eyes emphasized a common desire for paradise.

"Excuse me, baby."

A busty Asian lady in orange lingerie squeezed my elbow. She threw back her long black hair and continued down the aisle. A short slender Latina in a pink bodysuit followed. The women strolled with grace toward the group of men, greeting them with girly giggles and shoulder rubs. Both sat on two men's laps, stroking their thin hair and bald spots. The Asian lady took off one of the men's sunglasses and put them on her face. The Latina gripped the other man's blue tie, her plump butt gyrating within his groin. These "pretend kings" had the full attention of two pornstar goddesses. I wanted to live like them.

"Are y'all alive in here or what?" a female DJ shouted into a microphone from the corner booth. Her deep voice carried over the music. "This is DJ Trickster calling all tippers to the front. We're going to have another sexy dancer come on the stage in more ways than one."

After the small applause, I followed DJ Trickster's directions and moved to the front row, sitting near the center stage next to an older Asian man. His cigarette odor reeked of desperation. His dark sunglasses and thick gray beard covered most of his round face. He wore a black Helter Skelter shirt with Charles Manson's face on the front. The man grinned at me with his missing front tooth and then lifted up a coffee mug from his lap. The front read: I ♡ SLUTS.

"Will you teach me the ways of the force?" I asked with a smile.

"This is all me," he replied, ignoring my joke. His wrinkled finger pointed at the scattered bills on the stage. "Put food out early, they're not late to eat."

"What food? What you been eating?"

"Temptation." His two fingers pointed behind my shoulders. "Watch out."

My head turned slightly. At the corner of my eye was an older Black man with a pitiful Frederick Douglass afro sitting in the row behind mine. His arms hid within his large black trench coat, beneath his pants. His body jerked up and down rigorously in the chair. His parted mouth moaned. His blank eyes twitched and caught my glance. I retreated my attention forward.

"Alright deviants and disciples, time to get ready," D.J Trickster said and paused the music. "If dancing is like dreaming with your feet, then this next dancer will feel like a wet dream. We're going to slow it down with some Dawn Penn, 'You don't love me.' Y'all give it up to the beautiful and erotic...Siren!"

The lights dimmed to a blood red glow. A drum-roll rumbled the floor. A bass line *kicked, kicked, kicked* the soles of my shoes. A dreamy, saddened voice spoke in melody. I heard this voice before, long ago, at Maria's quinceañera of all places. Taniesha was teaching me the waltz, her first attempt. I remember her singing this melody into my ear.

"No, no, nooo..."

A tall woman with a light-brown complexion entered through the curtains. Her heavy make-up masked her youth. Her red stilettos announced her every step upon the stage. She strutted around the pole, greeting the audience to her red g-string. She took out a tissue and wiped the long pole. She rubbed the silver rod between her plump butt, laughing like a little schoolgirl. She tossed the tissue at the Asian man next to me. He put the wet wipe to his face, under his glasses, and then sniffed it deeply. He giggled. She giggled. They smiled in laughter. This "dancer" called Siren was everything true to her name. The music grew louder and louder as glimmers of my past shrunk thinner and thinner. Thoughts of Taniesha faded away. My heart lost all care of what was before.

"You don't love me, yes I know now, no, no, nooo..."

I watched Siren spin a short loop around the stage, one arm and leg tightly secured on the pole. Her body twirled in several circles, gradually turning upside down. Her tone legs opened, parting into the splits, and then closed, wrapping along the pole. With a quick swipe of her hand, she unhooked her red bra and squeezed her round breasts together, pinching her grape nipples. Her redbone body unhinged, still balanced upside down, facing my direction.

"No, no, nooo," Siren's voice overcame Dawn Penn's. "I'll do anything you say boy."

My heart paced. Her green eyes stared into mine. My palms sweated. Her long tongue flickered. My seat trembled from the tumbling bass. Her finger twirled as if casting a spell. When my pants constricted, her magic was near my limit. Nothing else mattered.

"Abandon every hope, ye who enter here," the Asian man said and pinched my arm.

"Too late."

CHAPTER 8

S aturday 1:31 a.m.

"Hello Mr. Bond, my name's Pussy Galore," a soft voice spoke into my ear.

A soothing hand squeezed on my bow tie, unloosening the knot. I turned my head to see a caramel goddess in red-lace lingerie standing behind my chair. Her curvy body moved around and stood in between my parted legs.

"Just kidding, you can call me Siren. I was eyeing you, eyeing me on stage."

"Who?" I surveyed the nearby empty seats of the Garden of Eden. "Me?"

"You're the only guy here in a penguin suit," Siren said and curled one finger to her nose. "So, there's a trick to that."

"A trick to *what*?" I asked and hid my bruised hands inside my pockets. "What are you talking about?"

"I used to be shy about eye contact too," Siren said as her plump breasts jiggled with each sudden move. "So, I tell boys who come here to look at the girl's nose. It's like you're staring into her eyes. You see, I'm doing it now. Alright, you try."

"I'm not shy. I'm cooler than a polar bear's toenails."

"You can turn off the charm, baby. I'm immune."

My gaze lifted from Siren's bra cleavage to her button nose. Her bright smile widened, revealing two round dimples upon her light-brown face. Her facial expression carried the innocence of a girl-next-door. Her tall statuesque body was built like a M.I.L.F porn star. I wanted to kiss her and know if her taste was better than Taniesha's.

"See Mr. Bond, I can't even tell," Siren said and winked. Then she pointed to my bandages and dried blood. "So, what's up with your hands? Did you fight a bear or something?"

"Yeah, something like that," I said and lowered my head. "Except they lost."

"I don't care what happened before. How about you tell me your real name?"

"*Name?*" I said, my body straightened up. "My real name is Jonah, Jonah Tarver."

"Okay, Jonah, *Jonah Tarver*," she said and leaned in closer. "Do you mind if I join you?"

"Yes, I mean no, I don't mind." I pointed at the open seat to my left, hoping she'd ignore my anxiety. "Sorry, please sit."

"You already passed the first test, so relax," she said with a wide smile. "*Woosah.*"

"What test?"

Siren's thin hands dived in between my legs, parting them slightly. Her toned arm stretched along my shoulder and then wrapped around my neck, engulfing my senses with her apple scented perfume. Her soft butt squatted. With ease, she sat in my lap. Her warm essence felt like baked bread resting on my thigh. The red g-string proved little purpose.

"Let's get sexy in this mothafucka," D.J Trickster announced into the microphone. She was hidden behind the corner booth. "We're going to slow it down with some 10cc 'I'm not in love.' Calling all tippers to the front."

"I'm not in love, I'm not in love!" shouted someone from the back row.

"Yeah buddy, keep telling yourself that," D.J Trickster replied. "Let's give a round of applause for our next dancer, who's Asian, from the far, far east...Miss Kimmy!"

A group of Asian men in the back row gave several claps that echoed throughout the empty strip club. The sunglasses man stood up with his coffee cup and yelled, "Where's the bitches?" One of his friends pulled on his shoulder, forcing him to return to his seat.

The music transitioned into a synthesized harmony, followed by a looping electric guitar, bass drum, and then an enchanted voice filled with melancholy.

"I'm not in love, so don't forget it, it's just a silly phase I'm going through..."

Behind my chair sat the old Black man with a gray Frederick Douglass afro. His arms and hands hid under his zipped-up army-fatigue trench coat. His grizzly head nodded in my direction, or maybe he was looking at Siren cuddled on my lap. Only he and God knew for sure.

"I like to see you, but then again, that doesn't mean you mean that much to me..."

The music grew louder, drowning the handclaps from the back row. Through the purple curtain, a busty Asian dancer strutted onto the stage. She tugged on her orange bra and thong, teasing the small crowd for a hungry applause.

"Go ahead, girl," Siren screamed. "Make that money, but don't let it make you."

Miss Kimmy waved back and continued toward the pole. Siren reached into her purse, took out a small bundle of bills, and threw the wad of cash onto the stage. She didn't bother to count it, nor did she care.

"You should give some tips too," she suggested and pointed to her donation. "You can get the money flowing, you know, and help out my girl. It's a slow night. How much you got?"

"I didn't really count, so I'm not sure." My hands searched each pocket, though reluctant to pull out my wallet. "But what's a normal tip? Like fifteen percent?"

"You don't know what's *really* going on, do you?" she asked. "Wait, how old are you?"

"I just turned eighteen. Tonight's my birthday."

"Holy shit!" she shouted and startled the hell out of me. Her arms wrapped around my body, straddling me tight in the chair. "There's still no cure for the common birthday."

"Why do people keep saying that?"

"Saying what? You're the one dressed up all GQ."

"My mama had said the same thing before I left for prom. It's been downhill ever since."

"Prom? I know you didn't go alone. Where's your date?"

"I don't know. Alive, I hope. No, I wish, I wish, I wish it was all a dream."

The bass drum and synth chords faded out. The music reduced into an acapella whisper.

"Be quiet, big boys don't cry, be quiet, big boys don't cry..."

My eyes shifted down to the purple neon bracelet still wrapped around on my wrist. *Why would you act like you cared?* The $9.99 beads and string was the last reminder of my first date with the one person whom I trusted as much as Keon. *I thought you loved me.* My eyes concentrated on the crimson-red carpet floor, but the darkness only brought back visions of prom. *Why would you fuck up everything?* I looked above at the flashing strobe lights, but then my *ex*-girlfriend appeared. Her body curled up on the bathroom floor, motionless.

"No, I did this," I whispered.

"What did you do?" she asked, but I shook my head.

My mind imagined Taniesha in the hospital. When she recovered, she would learn of my mental condition. She would discover that I had been without my medication for almost a month, secretly disposing of my pills. Yes, my girlfriend would understand. She would forgive me. She knew I wasn't a criminal nor did I deserve a life in jail. She loved me. I love her. I'll wake up from this madness. Everyone will be fine, but Trevon? I need to let go of the bracelet.

"I keep your picture upon the wall, it hides a nasty stain that's lying there..."

The music drifted on. Lingering sounds enabled a sudden loneliness. The song no longer motivated emotion. The emptiness had devoured my soul, leaving my body comfortably numb.

Siren snapped her fingers and stroked my chin. My attention shifted to her green eyes.

"Where'd you go?" she asked. "Is it past your bedtime, baby boy?"

"My name ain't boy. Don't call me that."

I rolled my eyes, then observed the whole room at a glance. The sunglasses man had made his way to the front stage, once again. Miss Kimmy was crouched down, displaying her opened legs for the man's amusement. Behind him were a group of Asian men in business suits, watching idly. The Black man with the Frederick Douglass afro sat alone quietly in the back row, covered by his trench coat. His arms and hands vibrated rigorously underneath his coat. His eyes focused on every motion of Miss Kimmy's body and then shifted toward my direction.

"What's his problem?" I asked then turned to Siren. "By the way, how old are you?"

"No, you can't do that," she replied and waved her manicured finger in my face. "I ask the questions first. So, where was I? Oh, out of all the places on earth, what brings your eighteen-year-old-ass to paradise?"

"I don't know."

"So why don't you know?" she asked and sat closer. "There's a reason for everything."

"Yes, but no, all I know is that I know nothing at all. One thing I do know for sure is *'In this narrow bed of earth, star-dust never scatters, and I tremble lest the darkness teach me that nothing matters.'* Oh shit, I got it right."

"Are you on one right now? What'd you take at the prom?"

"I don't know what I took, or even if I'm on anything anymore, but I do know those lines I said were from a Langston Hughes poem. Reciting them would always bring me back to the present somehow, especially when I feel super anxious and life becomes too much for me, which is like all the time. Maybe that was Keon's point in making me memorize the stupid poem, so I would understand loss. Damn, so much loss that I'm lost. You see, I did something really *really* bad at prom. Now I don't have anyone or anything anymore. I felt so lost before when Keon died, but now I feel even more lost."

"I hear you," Siren said and massaged my shoulder. "I see you and feel you, so let it go."

"I guess, I should've told you that Keon was my best friend. He was kind of like my big brother. He taught me the Hughes poem, but he died in a car accident four years ago. The same time as my birthday. His skull cracked open on the steering wheel. That's probably why I didn't go to his funeral, but no biggie. I'm talking too much. You said, 'let it go,' and that's what was on my mind, the ups and downs and turns, sometimes feels like..."

"Like a rollercoaster," Siren whispered and pressed her hand on my chest. "You have a good heart. And it's not like you're the first person to come in here not knowing what they want or where to go, and you damn sure ain't going to be the last. That's how the world is sometimes. So, you have to figure out your own happiness, your own way."

"I don't know. I guess, I'm starting to accept that whether or not happiness actually comes in this life, I have to be prepared to possibly live without it."

"So, what's the fun in that?" she asked, disarming me with her smile.

"Someone out there needs to chillax," D.J Trickster shouted, letting the music fade out. "We got one more song for Miss Kimmy. *Paging Wells.* Let's switch it up with some Nine Inch Nails. *Paging Wells to the back.* Y'all tippers do like the song says and get 'Closer.' *Yo Wells.*"

The music transitioned into a rumbling drum, snap, and synth followed a soft whisper:

"You let me desecrate you, you let me penetrate you, you let me complicate you..."

"Ah, '*Help me*,' yeah, this my shit," Miss Kimmy said to the sunglasses man. "Hold up, where you going, baby?"

"Help him," the man replied with disgust and pointed to the back row.

I watched the sunglasses man shake his head and retreat up the aisle. My body turned toward the back row and noticed the old Black man with his trench coat open. Something long, dark, and hard flopped around for all eyes to see. Then the music grew louder and disrupted the still room.

"I wanna fuck you like an animal, I wanna feel you from the inside..."

"Whoa, what's happening back there?" I asked. "You don't see that everyday."

"Have you ever played two truths and a lie?" Siren asked.

"No, I don't know. What's that?"

"It's okay if you haven't played it. It's simple. I'll say three facts about myself. You have to guess which one is false."

"Wait, wait, wait." I shook my head. "Did you just redirect me?"

"Ready?"

Siren ignored my question and raised up three fingers.

"One: I study Child Psychology at Cal Berkeley," she said. "Two: My real name is Naima, after a John Coltrane song." She paused and pointed her three fingers toward her crotch. "Three: My kitty has a habit of purring when excited. So, you've got five seconds. Go!"

"Wait, one, no, Naima is a fake. Whoa, what was three again?"

"Bzzzz," hummed from her mouth. She looked at her wrist and tapped her invisible watch. "Time's up. So, did you say Naima is fake? Actually, it's from a jazz ballad that Coltrane wrote for his wife."

"Naima, Naima. That's a beautiful name, but what does it mean?"

"It's Arabic for contentment."

"Are you Muslim?"

"Fuck no. That's just what the word means. Keep up. When you think about it, aren't we all trying to find contentment? Don't you want to be happy with life, have balance, feel good?"

"I don't know."

"What about being content with what happened?" she asked. "Have you ever thought that what has happened and will happen was just meant to be?"

"I don't know," I lied.

"You like to say that."

"Say what?"

"I don't know, I don't know," she mimicked. "I think you're just dodging the truth."

"I think you sound like my therapist. You don't know me."

"I know what worries you, will master you."

"Wells," D.J Trickster announced again over the microphone. *"Paging Wells."*

The music caught my ear. The 'Closer' song rang in my canals, relieving my doubts.

"I drink the honey inside your hive, you are the reason I stay alive..."

My lips quivered. My nose was runny. My eyes got watery. Deep breath. Hard gulp.

"Okay, if you really want to know the truth. It's all because I told my girlfriend, well, my *ex*-girlfriend, that I loved her. Then she went behind my back at the prom and destroyed everything. No. It was because I had a friend, a motherfucker I thought was my *best* friend, but fuck him. No. Fuck them both."

Woo-sah.

"I'm sorry if I get heated. It's weird. Sometimes I feel numb to the world. I pretend to be happy with the people I know. I don't want them to worry. They love me. I love them. But some days, it's like I'm on top of the world. Other days, when I'm really *really* low, I feel like a toilet bowl for the devil's diarrhea. The hardest part is what I can't control. Dr. Imani said that being bipolar can sometimes feel like riding a never-ending rollercoaster. After what happened to Keon, my world kind of felt pointless. Now I don't want to ride this rollercoaster anymore. I want to get off. Whew, that was so hard to say, but so easy to do."

"I get it," Naima said and nodded with approval. "So, did your therapist ever classify you as possibly having Cyclothymia?"

"Last time I checked, I didn't see any S.T.Ds," I replied.

"No, silly. I meant to say, do you have hypomanic episodes? You know, just like what you said, high and low days, weeks, or more like a rollercoaster. But now you got me curious. When was your last panic attack?"

"I don't know. I guess, well, about two hours ago. You see, I've been off my meds."

"Poor baby. Bless the heart who can bend, for he shall never feel broken."

"Hold up, how do you know all this? I thought you were just a..."

"Dancer? No, you never guessed the correct lie."

"Correct lie?"

The lobby door slammed shut, startling everyone in the dark room. Naima and I shifted our glances toward Wells marching down the aisle. The music faded away, overcome by the buff bouncer's heavy steps past the stage and toward the back row. He waved his hands, signaling everyone to move away, but Miss Kimmy hugged the pole and pointed to the front row.

"That's him!" she shouted.

Wells approached the old Black man and tapped his shoulder. The man jumped out his chair. Wells withdrew a few steps and crossed his arms as a shield. The man's trench coat flew open, revealing his erection through his unzipped pants. Miss Kimmy screamed louder than an actress in a horror film. The man whirled his penis around like a rubber dildo stuck to his zipper.

"This ain't that kind of party," Wells said.

The bouncer climbed over the back row chairs and held onto the old man's flailing arms.

"No, you got to go," he ordered.

"I just need to nut!" the man shouted, still resisting Wells' hold. "Wait, come on."

"No come on anything. You have to go now."

"I served, I served," he repeated and pointed to a U.S flag emblem on his coat. "I was in the army, bitch."

"Don't go there, I served too," Wells said, finally securing the old man's arms. "You know better than anyone, rules are rules."

"Nobody knows the troubles I've seen," he sang. *"Nobody knows but Jesus."*

Peacefully, Wells put his arm over the old man's shoulder and escorted him up the aisles. Both men disappeared through the exit door. The music resumed, switching to Sade's song, "The Sweetest Taboo."

From the back row, someone began singing off key, *"Is it a crime? Dun-dun-dun."*

"Nah friend, wrong song," D.J Trickster said, still hidden behind her booth. "Sorry about that. I guess some folks just can't keep their cock in the barn, but we're going to keep everybody happy, and keep the money rolling. So, we're offering two-for-one lap dances for the next hour. Yes, that's right, two dances for the price of one. You better find yourself a lucky lady now while the special is still hot, hot, hot like a December in Africa."

The music carried on with Sade's sultry voice calming the chaotic room.

"If I tell you, if I tell you now, will you keep on, will you keep on loving me?"

"So, what happened?" Naima asked with her hands to the side. "What you looking at?"

"You didn't see that? Some dude was jerking off."

I paused and watched her fingers slide several wads of cash into her purse.

"What are you doing, Naima?"

"What'd you say? Oh, you're cute," she said. "Has anyone shown you to the back room?"

"No, what back room?"

She pointed toward the dark path beyond the stage and then leaned closer for a tight hug. Her breasts squeezed against my chest. My penis swelled up thicker than a cucumber.

"The backroom is more intimate, more private for an XXX show," she whispered and winked. "You know, '*The Sweetest Taboo*' experience. I want you to want me to take care of you. So, how much cash you got, Mr. Jonah?"

"How much do I need, Ms. Naima?"

"Why did you call me that?"

"Wait, then which one was the lie?"

CHAPTER 9
MARKET

S aturday 2:07 a.m.

Market street reeked of piss, alcohol, and sin. Every corner displayed a pattern of vacant lights and closed gates. Each block revealed a row of shut doors and empty businesses. Normal people were away, probably sleeping. Normal people were busy with a booty call or inside a nearby bar after hours because normal people lived normal lives.

Normally, normal people weren't dressed in a tuxedo and bow tie, walking alone in downtown San Francisco at night, in search of an ATM to withdraw cash, so I can give to a dancer whose real name may or may not be from a John Coltrane song, so she could provide "The Sweetest Taboo" experience in the backroom of a strip club named after a Biblical paradise. Nothing about tonight felt normal, except reciting Langston Hughes' poem.

"But now I lie beneath cool loam, forgetting every dream..."

I stood on Market Street about to make my journey, but first decided to double check my wallet, counting my cash, and then storing all my belongings deep into my pockets. The Garden of Eden wouldn't accept my Bank of America savings card. Sonia, the cashier lady, had said that the walk was an easy five-minute stroll from the club to the bank. She offered Wells to come along as a security escort, as though I was too young to handle myself at night. I declined. This stranger and my parents shared the same belief and warning of staying careful every place I went. Honestly, others should be the ones *careful*.

I thought about my parents who would never admit to that truth, but I wasn't sure how they would react to any news up to this point. My mama would freak out from knowing that I had been inside a "titty disco" as she once described it. My father would likely abandon me. On top of all the other bullshit, he would probably turn me into the police if I tried to hide. This opportunity with Naima would probably be my last chance in a long time to experience a *real* woman. She was the contentment inside my paradise lost. In case this was my last night on earth, let me live content and lost in her paradise.

"And in this narrow bed of earth, no lights gleam."

My feet marched onward Market Street where the homeless occupied sidewalks like refugees without a country. Tattered tents and junk-filled shopping carts crowded my path. Sleeping zombies laid scattered on the concrete. I passed by a bald Latino man in gray overalls who snored louder than a congested bear. He wore no shoes or socks. His bloody feet were patched with torn newspaper. Where did his life go wrong? Why did he decide to give up?

This was home when you run out of homes.

When I was younger, I felt afraid of people like him. Once I had asked my mama where the homeless went when the sky rained. She laughed and said, "They aren't animals or pests." My father had told me most homeless were just lazy and without purpose. "Where there's a will, there's a way," he often reasoned. From then on, I developed my sort of hobo-phobia. Within my blindness, I saw the homeless as the living dead on earth. I was the fortunate fool. The error of heaven was that there were no more spaces.

Red light.

I stopped at the corner of Market and Larkin Street and closed my eyes. Within the darkness was hope for a divine intervention like a taxi or limo, maybe an angel or my family to rescue me. What if my mama, father, and little brother had arrived to pick me up like they did after a long day at school? What if I felt that comfort again, like when we would visit our favorite takeout place in Oakland?

"Who wants Nations?"

My father would order cheeseburgers for the whole family, except he and I would take everything on ours: onions, pickles, tomatoes, the works. My mama would decline her fries and share with Steven's portions in spite of his protest. On our drive back home, we'd listen to oldies and sing the lyrics at 80% accuracy. Everything everywhere was bliss. We were simple, so was life. Then came the loss of my best friend. The bipolar roller coaster. The tears kept hidden inside for so long. My eyes opened.

Green light.

On the corner I stood and stared at an old Black man across the street. He had wild wooly hair and wore a trench coat and brown army fatigue pants. I walked fast into the crosswalk with my head bowed. He marched closer in my direction. He looked like the old man with the Frederick Douglass afro who had gotten kicked out of the strip club. I kept glancing at the man, expecting he might jerk off on me from afar. We crossed paths. He stopped. My feet continued walking. He turned around and followed me to the corner.

"Young blood," the man said and waved his arms like an air-traffic signaler. "Be still."

"That *is* him," I said aloud and slapped my forehead. "What do I do?"

"Young blood, be still," he repeated, a little louder. "Let me speak to you right quick."

I shook my hands. "No thanks. I have to go."

There were only a few seconds to flee, but to run meant possibly going the wrong direction, getting lost in San Francisco, losing my chance to experience Naima. Yet for some reason, my eyes retreated to the ground. On the concrete lay a large brown cockroach on its back. The pest's tiny legs and antennas twitched in the air. Both the roach and man studied me.

"That's a mighty fine zoot suit," the man said from a few feet away. He was admiring my tuxedo jacket. "Be still, let me talk to you."

"Thanks, but no thanks."

My mind imagined performing a karate chop, or some kind of defense move on the old man, if only I knew one. My window for escape had closed. I dug my hand into my pocket and jiggled the car key.

Not sharp enough.

"Like I said, I need to go, sir."

"Don't call me *sir*," the old man said. "Name's Pater."

"Pater?" I said his name slowly, "*Pa-ter, Pa-ter* doesn't that mean father or something?"

"What's your name?" Pater asked, ignoring my question.

"*Name?* My name is, is, is Trevon. Why do you want to know?"

"Well, ain't this a coincidence." He loosened his trench coat. "Hold up, be still, boy."

"Why do you keep saying that? What do you want?"

"You Trevon, last name's Ellison? Nah, why would it? Long time ago, I served with Trevon Ellison in my unit. A funny guy too. A young blood like yourself. He told all sorts of jokes to the boys in my bunker. Tre had this one joke he used to say all the time. Let me think, it's a limerick." He paused and scratched his gray hair. *"There once...oh, okay...There once was a man from Nantucket, whose dick was so long he could suck it, he said with a grin, while wiping his chin, if my ear was a cunt I would fuck it!"*

Pater erupted in laughter. He spit with each chuckle and slapped my arm between breaths. My body flinched then froze. A sudden silence stood between us. The streets felt empty. No sign of traffic. For a moment, I thought that this crazy vet and I were the only people left alive in the world. The mere possibility of such an idea made my body numb with fear.

"Thanks for the joke, but I have to go," I mumbled and stared down Market Street.

"Tre was a poor bastard," Pater continued and shook his head in shame. He wiped saliva from his chin. "Young blood had about a hundred versions of that limerick. Our lieutenant cracked up every time. Poor bastard got it bad though when we left Da Nang. This sonofabitch, Melvin tripped on a landmine. He blew himself half to shit. Tre was marching right behind that fucker. Shrapnel tore up his pupils. The blast blew out his eardrums. He couldn't see or hear. After nine months in rehab, he got shipped back, blind and deaf at twenty-one. Only joke left was him bragging about being the number one pussy eater on the base. That was all Tre could do, all he could do, and you know what?

That's when it hit me. Life is like glass. Strong men like P.F.C Ellison are as fragile as glass, fucking beautiful until broken."

"Well, okay, I'm sorry to hear that about Trevon, but there's somewhere I need to be."

He reached for my arm and then pointed to the stamp on my wrist.

"I seen't you at the Garden of Eden," he said. "You were there, huh? Don't lie."

"Maybe, but didn't you get kicked out of there for like doing something *something* in the back row?"

Why did I ask another question? Why did I not walk, leave, and disappear? My mind had all these thoughts of not staying. However, worry and fear prevented my body from doing anything other than nod, grin, and listen to this strange veteran with a Frederick Douglass afro.

"I served in Nam for four damn years," Pater said and rubbed on the U.S flag emblem stitched on his sleeve. "You think they care, huh? They kicked me out of the V.A with nowhere to go. So now the state just calls me 'unhoused,' like I'm looking for a better home."

The old man's hoarse voice had awakened some nearby homeless in rolled blankets. Their wrapped bodies quivered on the sidewalk like stirring caterpillars. Oblivious of his surroundings, Pater spat onto the sidewalk, and then stood still, staring down at the same roach I had noticed earlier. The brown pest, no bigger than a silver dollar, began to roll on its tiny legs, attempting to run and escape for dear life. Pater stomped on the roach with his green boot.

"They let Monsanto spray chemtrails over South Nam," he continued shouting. "You know they infected them gooks with Agent Orange. Nixon fucked them kids up and turned them into deformed inbreds. Reagan and Nancy were a bunch of hypocrites. And fuck Hinckley; his ass should have gotten it right the first time. Nah, they care about their good ol' boys when they're serving, but when we ain't in no war, the bottomline is this: What you know about surviving, huh? You ever eaten roaches to survive, boy?"

"No, I don't think I have, and my name ain't boy."

"Who do you think you are?" Pater replied.

"I am who I am, I think."

I took a step back. His yellow teeth grinned then hissed.

"I know what you all about," he said. "You ain't fooling nobody, boy."

"I'm nobody's *boy*."

"Don't you see? It's all in your face, clothes, and your talk." He gritted his teeth and pointed to my tuxedo. "I seen't bougie guys like you before. You got everything handed to you on a silver spoon. You got a full life, but ain't grateful for nothing."

"In this narrow bed of earth," I paused, trying to recollect. *"Star, stardust never..."*

"You figure it ain't no point, so you're trying to escape life, live a fantasy, but you really just afraid, huh? You're scared of reality, huh? You're terrified how it's all gonna end, huh?"

"No, wait a second, *and I,* wait, *stardust never scatters, and I*...ah, fuck."

"The Lord's near to the brokenhearted, and saves those who are crushed in spirit."

"Oh my God, what am I doing?"

"No, the real question you need to ask ain't where you're going, what you're doing, why you're here. It's really about how you live, how you treat others. You know God sees everything. Jesus would want you to help me. Oh, that reminds me." He paused and searched his pants' pockets. "Let me show you something. Wait a minute."

My feet were inactive. My legs were locked in place.

"No, no, I have to go, really."

"This here is Abraham and Magdalene."

Pater held up a worn polaroid of two children. His finger tapped on a small boy in a blue polo shirt, and then onto a young girl in a green dress. Both kids weren't smiling.

"I call them Abby and Maggy. Them my pride and joy."

Behind was the Bank of America on the next block.

"Nice picture. A work of art. Really, will you excuse me?"

"They're in Texas," he blurted and stared at the photograph. "I know what you're thinking. I got a plan. It's been years, but I'm going to buy a ticket to Dallas and surprise my kids. Just tonight was bad. I was so down and lonely. You know how it is. You can't blame an old man for wanting to see some ass. It cost me my last twenty, even with the Vet discount. I haven't seen a G.I check in three months. I need a little bit to hold me over. You know what I'm saying, Trevon, so like five dollars?"

I raised up five fingers. "You want five dollars?"

"Like five dollars," he said.

"Wait, all of that was for like *five dollars?*"

"Five dollars," he repeated and smiled.

I shook my head, took out my wallet, and gave Pater four dollars and eighty-five cents.

"Thank you, Trevon," he said.

I watched him count the money, stuffed the cash and coins into his back pocket, and then picked up his trench coat from the ground.

I gave a salute. "Goodbye."

"You never say goodbye. Always see you later."

Pater bowed and stood silently on the corner. He watched my attempt to walk normally across the street. Our entire conversation replayed through my mind with each distancing step. Somehow, this stranger knew I was trying to escape. I have been running away from my troubles since I was thirteen, the morning I heard about Keon's death, and then later in the bathroom.

Sirens.

My thoughts got interrupted by a fire truck speeding through the lane, driving too fast for me to jump on and hitch a ride. The traffic lights flashed on and off and then back to green. I turned and glanced back at the corner.

The old man was nowhere in sight, perhaps searching for his next five dollars.

See you later.

When I got to the corner of the Bank of America, I noticed four Black guys in black pea-coats standing behind a bus stop booth. They huddled in a tight circle and smoked from a long fat cigar. As I passed by, I was engulfed by a thick hazy fog with a loud grassy aroma. Each man stood on guard like the four horsemen of the apocalypse, except instead of horses, they had on Jordans.

"What's the difference between Sativa and Indica?" the bald, heavy guy asked.

He exhaled a deep breath of smoke. He had a robust body and round-chocolate face similar to Notorious B.I.G.

"This Kush got a nigga's brain on lean," he said. "I'm itching for something to pop off."

Keep walking.

"That nigga's hella suited," said a skinny guy with long dreads.

He smacked the arm of his light-skinned friend with a short messy afro. Both guys cupped their hands over their mouths and called out in unison.

"Where the butt-naked hoes at?"

Be silent.

"Hold up a sec." The tall one with wavy hair pointed at me. "I swear I know that nigga."

Stay deaf.

Under a looming gray cloud, all four guys snickered and chuckled in my direction. My feet switched into speed-walk mode, marching past the Black men like a panicked white lady. Their eyes followed my every step. My mind thought about Raymond and our conversation at prom. His warning about Blacks and niggas, and how he put it: "Niggas ruin shit for everyone." Born Black and raised in Oakland gave me no right to prejudge. Yet my spidey-senses were telling me to get the hell out of dodge.

No turning back.

I hurried over to the brightly lit ATM and moved in closer to the machine. My right hand slid the card while my left hand covered the keypad. Both index fingers typed in my pin.

The screen read: SPECIFY YOUR WITHDRAWAL AMOUNT.

100. 200. 300. OTHER.

This account was my only line for money. My father instructed me to keep my savings "safe" in case of an emergency. What would he think of his "boy" now? His "boy" needed the money safely in his hands, so that he could have his chance with a dancer named Naima.

She is my contentment.

I would do whatever necessary to have her, touch her, feel her. This brown skin goddess would provide the happiness I had been searching for. My heart had nothing left to lose. So now urgency became an emergency.

My finger pressed in the amount. My eyes watched as fifteen $20 dollar bills dropped into a stacked pile. My hands grabbed the cash.

"What up playa."

I froze in place like a frightened deer. When I turned around, the tall guy and the heavy one stood a few feet away. Both men waved the peace sign.

"Don't I know you?" the tall one asked. Under his right eye was a tattooed teardrop.

"I don't think so," I replied, still frozen in place.

"Nah, I seen't you before," he said and nodded.

"Stop playing, bruh," the heavy guy told him. "You really know this bougie-ass, James Bond-looking nigga? Check out his hands though. Looks like he was finger-banging a blender."

"Hold up, who's James Bond?" whispered the skinny guy in the back.

"Google it nigga," he told him.

The heavy guy crossed his arms and stared at my Stacey Adams shoes. I ignored his glossy eyes as well as the cold glare from the other two guys behind them. They blocked my route back to paradise. My keys and karate chop were useless.

I wish I had my father's gun.

"Hey, you run track?" the tall guy asked. "Yeah, I seen't you before, running at the Berkeley meet a few years back. Didn't you know Keon?"

"Who?" I asked.

"Keon."

The name struck my ears. As much as I tried blocking out my best friend's memory, he always seemed to come up no matter what I did. At eighteen, he was like the mature brother I never had. At thirteen, I was the immature boy too afraid to go to his big bruh's funeral. Now that I've turned eighteen, I wasn't sure if I would live longer than he did.

"Keon," I whispered.

"Yep, that's how I know you," the tall guy said. "You remember eating at that one Denny's on Hegenberger hella years ago? Bruh, you was sitting right across from me with Keon. I thought y'all two were brothers. Damn, you was just a little nigga back then."

"My name is Jonah."

"Jonah, Jonah, yeah I ain't forget you," he said with a wide smile, revealing two gold-fronts. "Ain't this a God-damn coincidence. You don't remember me? It's Wice, but like wise with a C, you dig. And this my nigga Big O like the tires."

"I'm feeling them shoes." Big O pointed to my Stacey Adams. "What size is those?"

"My size," I replied.

"Chill my nigga," Wice told Big O. "This folks right here. Me and his big bruh go way back." He turned and gave me dap. "You was like a freshman when I saw you, right? How old is you now?"

My eyes felt the heavy glares from the three other guys huddled around. I traded glances with Big O, still staring at my shoes.

"I just turned eighteen. Tonight's my birthday. I was supposed to be at my prom."

"For real? But how come you here though?" Wice asked.

"I don't really know where here is anymore."

"You know Keon would've said: Still ain't no cure to the common birthday." Wice paused and stared at the ground. "I would always tell that nigga chill with all them quotes, especially them lines from Hughes. You know that one poem I'm talking about? Shit was called..."

"Teacher," I interrupted. "How did you know Keon?"

"Me and him used to party it up, slaying hella hoes back when I went to school, you know, before I decided I was finished. He tried hyping me up on going to college like him, but school ain't for everybody. Don't know how he balanced straight A's and stayed hella on one. He was faded like almost every weekend, but ain't let nobody know his dirt, until he fucked up that night from cruising hella lit."

"Hella lit? Wait, what are you talking about? No, wait, no one told me that. That's not how he died. No one said anything like that. Keon didn't drink or do drugs, especially not when driving. No, he wasn't like that."

"I guess, you ain't know Keon," he said and shook his head. "He was hella-*ella* lit. I was there before it happened. Shit, I was there when they buried him. You even go to his funeral?"

"No, I was too scared." I paused and let out a sigh. "I wish I had gone."

"Don't trip bruh," Wice said and paused. He studied the cracks in the concrete. "When I heard he was gone, I was fucked up, for real. He was going to be somebody. Then the old God pulled his card, just like that. I mean, they be saying the good die young, but it still ain't right, not at eighteen. It's like this life shit don't be having no point."

"For my niggas," the skinny guy said and tipped his red cup.

Liquid poured onto the sidewalk. Everyone bowed their heads in silence.

I forced a smile. "Man plans. God laughs."

"Hold, hold up," the light-skinned guy called out. "What the fuck you mean?"

"So like man plans. God is a comedian. You know what? Forget I said anything."

"Why is you acting like you know shit?" the light-skinned guy said and stepped closer. "My cuzzo got murked last month. Dare your ass to say that bullshit in front of his niggas."

"Yo Draco, chill," Wice ordered. He took the blunt from his friend who still appeared rattled. "I get what lil' bruh is saying though. But Keon would've said something like true death arrives when the last person to remember you dies."

No one else said a word after that. Wice puffed on the blunt and stared blankly at the ground. Big O gulped from his red cup and watched my motions. A silence lingered beyond a moment as seconds felt like minutes.

What am I doing? Where can I escape?

Polk street was clear on my left, no traffic. I figured I could've sprinted around the corner, maybe run along the side avenues, and then I would return on Market Street toward the back entrance of Garden of Eden. That was the intention, but worry and fear imagined these four guys following me, harassing me, jumping me, or worse.

"So what's good, bruh?" Wice asked and passed the blunt to Big O. "We about to do some bips right quick, so what dirt you trying to get into? You want to cop something, my nigga?"

"What dirt? I ain't no cop, and my name ain't nigga. It's Jonah."

"Look, ain't nobody going to no ATM at two in the morning so they can buy a Bible."

"Hotel Bibles are free, but honestly, I'm about to go see someone, a woman for *'The Sweetest Taboo'* experience, whatever that means."

"Ahhh, *sookie sookie* now. You about to smash some pro, huh? Listen, I got some good shit for you. I got that fetti, that x, that white, and that greenery too. I got whatever to make them bitches hella on one and nasty. Hold up, is you on one right now?"

"I don't think so." The words slurred from my tongue. "I don't know."

"He hella lame though," Big O said and laughed, releasing smoke with each chuckle. In turn, the whole group erupted into laughter. "You trying to buy or not, little nigga?"

"Look, my name is *Jonah*," I said and noticed a grin appear on Big O's dark brown face.

"For real though," Wice interrupted and stepped closer with his fists clenched. "If we wasn't cool from way back, my nigga O would've been had you shook. We being polite as fuck right now, so what's *really* good bruh?"

The sudden worry and fear pushed me to consider something my former self never would. I wondered if Naima smoked weed. Taniesha said she never did drugs. I really knew nothing about her, or anyone for that matter. I could no longer dwell upon people who couldn't change. One must leave the past behind, sparing no space for regrets. I had become someone new, the man who cared less.

"How much for some trees?" I asked.

"How much you got?" Wice replied and smirked. "You ain't got to lie to kick it."

"Yeah bruh, we saw you pull out about a rack," Big O added.

I measured an inch with my fingers.

"I just want a little bit, you know, enough for a blunt."

"I'm going to hook you up with a dub, since we go back," Wice said. "You got thirty?"

"Yeah, I think so." I reached into my wallet. "What's a dub?"

"One sec," he said. "A homeless nigga coming."

Wice pointed to someone crossing the street. All four guys turned toward the old man with an afro like Frederick Douglass.

Did Pater follow me?

The pea-coat group bunched together upon noticing the old man. Pater ran toward our direction with his hands up as though to signal peace. His trench coat was missing. His green pants were unzipped. Wice turned his back to Pater and exchanged his bag of weed with the cash from my hand. I tucked the weed inside my coat pocket. However, the discretion didn't matter. Pater's locked eyes had witnessed the entire trade.

"Trevon, what are you doing?" Pater asked me. "This ain't who you are, son."

"Who this old nigga talking to?" Wice asked. "Ain't no Trevon up in here."

"Pater is cool," I said and stepped to his side. "Leave him alone."

"Don't tell me you know this homeless nigga?" he said and laughed. "Bruh, you need better friends."

Wice nodded to Big O who nodded to the other two guys. All three stood on guard with their hands in their coat pockets. Wice gave a final nod and then pointed at me.

"Let him be," I said. "He's no trouble."

"What's he saying?" Pater asked me. His brown eyes sunken with sadness. "Why'd you lie to me? Who are you really?"

"I don't know."

My arms had a sudden urge to hug the old man, but instead, I just stood still.

"Nah, real shit is popping off here, old dude," Wice told Pater and pointed toward Market Street. "No shade or what not, but you need to get like a ball and bounce."

"Young blood," Pater said and extended his hand to Wice, but he resisted. "Be still."

"Be what? Nah, fuck that."

Wice pounded his right fist into his left palm. His shoulders tensed up. His legs parted. Soon his whole body took on a boxing stance.

"I know this mop-head nigga ain't trying to square up," Wice said. "You best step off."

Big O and the other two guys huddled around both Wice and Pater, almost squeezing me out from their circle. I stood detached, watching the young man square up with an old veteran who was maybe three times his age.

"Be still," Pater ordered with his bearded chin held up. "Listen, I'm in the army, bitch."

"Like I give a fuck you in the army or NASA," Wice said and pushed Pater's shoulder. "I said you best step off before I make you my son in front of old God."

"Watch your mouth of blasphemy," Pater replied. "Don't swear on the Lord's name. He hangs on our every word."

"Bitch, I'm hung like Jesus," he proclaimed.

My body stood motionless. My eyes watched Pater move away from Wice's reach. His right arm lifted. He blocked Wice's punch and then elbowed his back as he fell forward.

"This is God's work," Pater said and put Wice into a chokehold.

"Oh, hell nah," Big O said and dropped his red cup. "Let's fuck this nigga up."

Big O charged at Pater like an angered linebacker to Wice's defense. All three men wrestled one another, eventually colliding into the wall by the ATM. Big O moved behind Pater and kicked his back leg. The other two guys jumped into the primal fight. Both attempted to hold onto Pater's arms. The old man tugged free and jumped onto Wice. Pater sunk his teeth into Wice's neck, before falling to the ground.

"What the fuck!" Wice screamed and pressed on his neck. "This nigga just bit me!"

Pater bent his knee. His head tilted back. His arms raised to the sky.

"Our father in heaven," Pater recited and bowed his head. *"Hallowed be your name..."*

"What's that mumbo jumbo?" Draco asked. "He's on some voodoo shit."

"Your kingdom come, your will be done on earth as it is in heaven!"

"Grab that glass," Wice ordered, limping like a hunchback. "Bust his head open."

Big O picked up a beer bottle from the trash can. He rushed behind Pater and smashed the bottle against the back of his skull. The glass shattered to pieces. The impact brought Pater's body to the ground.

Big O turned to Wice. "You alright?"

"Fuck you mean, *you alright*?" Wice said and pointed at his wet neck. "This homeless nigga just gave me AIDS. I ain't got no insurance for that shit. Nah, stomp that nigga out."

Wice planted his foot onto Pater's back. The other three guys immediately followed by enlisting a fury of kicks into the poor man's body. Pater resisted for a while, curling up into a fetal position. When the guys stepped on his legs and crotch, his defenses were soon destroyed. Wice rubbed his Jordan shoe against the old man's neck, leaving a dirt mark on his bloody skin.

"You did this," Wice told Pater and then nodded to his group. "Y'all know what's up. Check if he's holding,"

"Fasho, I got you," Draco said.

He searched Pater's pockets in spite of no protest. Within seconds, he pulled out a four-dollars and some pictures.

"He ain't got shit but some ugly-ass photos," he concluded.

"Oh hell nah, let's dip," Big O said.

As if a gun had popped, all four guys sprinted off one by one up Polk street.

"See you later," a voice called.

Sirens screamed in the distance, maybe an ambulance, or a police car, or someone else who could lend compassion where I couldn't. The sidewalk was filled with shattered glass and scattered photos of an old man's past. Though my back was turned, I could hear Pater groaning for pity, somehow reminding me of Trevon in that bathroom. The desire to help couldn't overcome my fear of the consequences.

The sirens grew louder and closer. Paradise awaited, leaving no time for empathy. A green light appeared on Market Street like a feeling of déjà vu.

"Tre."

CHAPTER 10
SiReN

S aturday 3:13 a.m.

"We're all just like micro-bees because God is a scientist."

My voice echoed inside the bathroom stall. Gray smoke carried the words out my mouth.

"It's microbes," Naima corrected me. "What's your point?"

She grabbed the burning blunt from my fingers, pressed it to her glossy pink lips, and took short puffs.

"What if we're all in this like a huge, little pastry dish?" I asked. "Imagine this super small pastry dish that's trapped inside of this big-ass storage tank. Let's call it the universe, or better yet, let's call it a lab experiment like the one I did in Mr. Camus' Bio class. I remember we scraped the inside of our mouths with a Q-Tip and dipped it into a pastry dish. At first, the bacteria was like this little millimeter speck. Then after like two weeks, it grew into this yellow splotch the size of a dime. Under the microscope we saw all sorts of little mini-thingy things moving around like some kids on a playground. Then it hit me: That's how the universe was formed. No big bang, just a big-ass plastic container, but that would mean no heaven or hell, or reincarnation. What if there's nothing after death? It's kind of scary like there's no point to it all. I don't even remember what happened when the experiment was over. I think Mr. Camus ended up throwing away all those pastry dishes."

"Petri," Naima interrupted. Smoke parted from her lips.

"What?" I asked.

"You kept saying pastry dish," she said and took another puff. "But it's *petri* dish."

"Petri...petri," I repeated. "Sounds like a peach tree. A petri. Do you like peaches? I do."

Naima shook her head. A frown filled her brown face. She stood on the toilet lid, holding onto my shoulder for balance. She lifted up the bathroom window and howled at the full moon. A cloud of smoke escaped into the moonlight.

"What's your favorite fruit then?" I asked.

"Apples," she said and giggled.

"Like Eve? My grandma said Eve cursed women for eternity with periods, but don't nobody want to blame Adam for nothing."

"You're funny when you're high."

"I never smoked weed before. How do you know I'm high?"

She blew the ashes into the toilet before offering me a puff.

"Siren always knows," she said. "Lucky for you, I had a blunt wrap in my locker."

I grabbed the lit blunt with hesitation. My eyes sunk into the small orange flame.

"I never smoked weed before."

"You said that already," she said. "This shit is dank."

She stepped off the toilet, brushed debris off her breasts. and adjusted her red bra. The smoke created a misty aura above her head like a halo.

"Sorry, what's *dank*? I'm kinda lame. Honestly, I didn't think you would be into weed."

She shook her head and watched my hand holding the blunt.

"This makes up for the long ass wait," she said. "So, what were you doing that whole time? Did you get a sudden change of heart?"

"You wouldn't believe what happened to me on Market Street. It was like a jungle out there that made me wonder how I've kept from going under, but I'll tell you about it later, or next time I guess, if there is a next time."

"That's why they call it, Market." She pointed to my hand. "So, the blunt's lit."

"By the way," I interrupted her with a sudden thought. "Are you sure we're not going to get caught smoking in the ladies' bathroom? Last time I was in the bathroom was..."

"Not a lot of girls come to the club. Most folks use this one to fool around, so listen."

"Fool around?" I interrupted again. "As in like sex?"

"So, you going to talk or smoke?"

With a nod and a grin, I inhaled a deep puff from the blunt. I closed my eyes and held in the smoke for as long as I could. My mind grew crowded with thoughts of my grandparents who died from lung cancer, the warnings to "STAY DRUG-FREE" from my father, and Keon's car accident from driving "hella lit," according to Wice. When I exhaled, a thick fog escaped my mouth, followed by cough, after cough, after cough. My body erupted in spasms.

"It's okay, coughing makes you higher."

She patted my back. I coughed more. She grabbed the blunt and stood beside the toilet. Her green eyes were filled with fright.

"Oh shit, are you okay?" she asked.

"Fine, I'm fine," I repeated and rushed out the stall. "I'll be back."

The door slammed shut right before my eyes. The bathroom grew gray. A white orb hovered above the sink light. Inside the square mirror reflected a Black boy in a tuxedo. He spoke. No sound escaped his mouth. The faucet vomited a stream of water. The boy moved. No action inspired his body. The sink overflowed past the brim. A river splashed onto the crimson ground. The stream spread past the boy's shoes and shadow. The water creeped toward a Black girl in a blue dress asleep on the floor. Her bloody body submerged under a low sea. She didn't wake up. The whisper of her slumber rippled the waves. The boy listened. His ears couldn't hear.

"Please don't do this."

The toilet flushed.

"Did you say something?" Naima asked.

She stepped out from the bathroom stall and turned off the running faucet.

"You almost drowned us," she said. "You alright? That was a strong hit."

Some sort of euphoria lifted my body. A smile stretched along my face.

"I feel pretty damn good. I can't feel my face though. But hey, that's not a big deal. I feel alive, much better than before when I was talking my ass off earlier. I probably said some stuff I shouldn't have like being bipolar and the whole rollercoaster deal. Honestly, nobody except my family knows that stuff. I told you the truth because, well I think, I might be in love with you."

She pulled my hand onto her breasts. Her soft voice whispered into my ear.

"Do you want me to keep you company?" she asked.

"Yes, I want you. I want your company for as long as I can."

She blew a kiss and then pointed to the door. My head nodded almost automatically.

"Follow me."

Naima and I walked out the bathroom, passing the lobby booth and the cashier lady. Sonia was too busy on her phone to pay us any attention. I pulled back the purple curtain, allowing Naima to enter the main room where we first met.

"Stay close."

My body followed her every step. Her gentle stride floated down the aisle. My gaze was hypnotized by her red bra and thong barely containing her coke-bottle silhouette. When she turned, her green eyes looked into mine. We smiled at the same time, enamored in bliss as Rick James' song, "Give it to me baby" played in the background.

"When I was high as the sky, out all night just dancing..."

The strip club was barely empty. Strobe lights danced along a vacant stage. The group of Asian men from earlier had disappeared. Only two Latino men in denim overalls were present in the front row. Their lonely eyes watched Naima and I skipping to Rick James' serenade.

"I say 'Wait til I squeeze you,' maybe then you'll start groovin'..."

Naima led my hand past another purple curtain. We marched through a dark hallway with several closed doors. The rooms were labeled with different Roman numerals. Deep moaning and panting echoed behind the V door. A porno might have been filming only inches from us. We stopped at the last door labeled X. Naima propped the door open and signaled me to step inside. Her light green eyes casted a spell, enchanted by Rick James' voice.

"Give it to me baby, I betcha I'll make ya hot like you had enough..."

Once we entered the cramp room, the outside music faded into a murmur. I stood next to a sofa chair and nightstand, both facing a tall mirror. On the side wall was a mounted black device with a card swiper and a deposit slot. The machine had a small bright screen that flashed: CASH OR CREDIT. A green light appeared above the door.

"Sit down baby," she said. "Siren's going to take care of you."

When she pointed to the chair, I obeyed and sat down like a true pet.

"I just need love. Will you love me?"

Naima nodded and stood between my parted legs. She pressed her round breasts into my face and caressed my hair with smooth long strokes. With each brush, my heart nearly skipped a beat. Her plump body straddled my lap in the sofa chair. Though shy at first, my hands lowered from her slender back and drifted in between her thick thighs.

"So, you remember what we talked about earlier, right?" she asked.

I nodded as if I knew what she was talking about.

"I'll need the donation, okay."

Naima's body leaned into mine. A faint apple scent tickled my nose. Her wet lips sucked on my earlobe. Her soft fingers groped my shirt and snuck through an open button, caressing my stomach. Her warm hands parted from my center but continued roaming lower. One hand searched my pocket. The other tugged on my crotch. Her left hand retracted from my pockets, revealing a fist full of dollars. Her right hand gave a gentle pat on my stiff member. Her face smiled with innocence. Her finger pointed at the wall device.

"So, this is for the room," she said. "I'm going to put your money in here, okay."

"Yes, anything you say." I submitted and then pointed to the black device. "It looks like one of those machines they have at Dave-n-Busters."

"So, money goes to the house, and every minute counts," she said with a sigh and raised up from my lap. "Don't worry, I'll do it for you, and I'll add just a little tip, okay?"

My head nodded and watched Naima insert several bills into the device one at a time. She placed a few bills into her Coach bag purse and then pulled out a glossy red condom. A red light flashed above the door.

"What was that?"

"What was *what*?" She ignored my question. "Empty your pockets, baby."

Under her sharp stare, I placed my keys, watch, wallet, and phone onto the nightstand. I took off the bracelet with Taniesha's name and tucked it into my back pocket.

For some reason, my conscience told me to keep the gift separated.

"I don't want anything in the way," she said. "Now take off your clothes, baby."

"Yes, anything for you."

Naima tore open the condom and moved closer. She took off my jacket, unknotted my bow tie, unbuttoned my shirt, loosened my belt, and unzipped my pants. Naima pointed to my shoes and socks as if to remove them myself, which I did, and then she threw all my clothes to the corner.

"You want to fuck?" she asked, pinching the condom with two fingers.

I reached for her open hand. She flinched.

"I need to feel loved."

Naima nodded and placed the condom over her lips. She pulled down her red thong. The thin cloth dropped to her ankles. A smooth triangle shave pointed to her love below. She bowed to my lap where I must have had the biggest erection in my life. Her wet lips worked the tight plastic on my third leg. I reached for her bra strap. She smacked my hand. I kissed her hair. She moved away and pushed me back.

"No," she said.

Naima jumped onto my lap. Her eyes closed. She licked her fingers and massaged between her brown thighs. The other hand danced onto my chest and moved below, slowly teasing and stroking me. My moans vibrated into begs. She pulled me inside her warmth. Our bodies thrusted together so deeply that I felt her heartbeat.

Is this real love?

She leaned all her weight onto my chest. Her nails dug deep into my shoulder. Her thick body bounced up, down, back, and forth, cramping my legs.

"Tell me you love it baby," she ordered and moaned like a pornstar.

"Yes, I love it so much. I love you Naima. I love you."

"Stop calling me that. Just fuck me. Cum, cum for me baby."

The black device beeped twice. The red light above the door flashed on and off.

"Kiss me, please," I pleaded while pulling her close. "I love you."

"I don't kiss on the lips." She turned the other cheek. "I'll kiss you in other places."

"But I love you."

"You got two minutes."

"Do you love me?"

"Hurry up and cum."

Smacking rubber echoed throughout the musty room. Her heavy hips straddled my lap like a loose horse saddle. Her fleshy stomach had stretch marks and needle wounds. A fish smell arose from her spiky, shaved groin. Her faded make-up had sweated off any remaining allure.

"What happened?" she asked and tried to kiss my neck. "You lost it."

"Sorry, I don't know," I lied and turned my head to the side.

"Okay, but if you want to keep this going, put another twenty in the machine. Otherwise, you can stay here and finish yourself off. It's whatever nigga."

"No, don't do that. Can you please wait? Let's talk at least."

She sat up from my lap and pulled me out of her like an overdue tampon. The black device stopped beeping. The light above the door turned green. In a haste, she rummaged through the nightstand and stuffed her belongings into her purse.

"Look, little boy." She rolled her eyes. "You got any more money or not?"

I reached for her cold hand, but she swatted my attempts.

"I don't know. Wait Naima, why are you acting like this? What's wrong?"

"Nah nigga, what's wrong with *you*? You're wasting my time with that 'I don't know' bullshit. Fuck is wrong with you, boy."

"There's nothing's wrong with me. Don't say that. I thought you understood me, Naima."

"No, my *name* is Siren."

She didn't say anything after that. She let her actions do all the talking. She sealed up her bulky purse and got dressed in less than a minute. She left the room without one glance back at the poor sucker she lured in.

"I wanted to be a good man, though I pinched my soul."

I pulled off the moist condom and dropped the mistake behind the chair. My body walked to the mirror and saw a naked Black boy. *Am I sick?* But no illness was far more destructive than lust. The rejection had hurt more knowing Naima, Siren, or whatever her name was, probably never gave a damn about me from the beginning. My only solution was to escape somewhere far, but my watch, phone, and keys were gone.

"Where's my shit?"

Breathe. I searched behind the chair, around the nightstand, each corner of the cramped room. *Breathe.* I collected my wallet and skimmed through it, not once or twice. Six times. *Breathe.* My emotions clouded my conscience again. I needed to find this thieving-ass bitch.

"*Woosah,* Jonah, *woo-sah,*" I told myself and then roared. "Nah, fuck that."

I pulled up my pants and buttoned my shirt halfway. I put on my socks inside out and slipped into my untied shoes. My hands held onto my jacket, and bow tie, and then sprinted out the back room. My feet ran through the narrow hallway and opened the doors to loud music.

"I don't want yo' man 'cause I got it like that, but it ain't even gotta be like that..."

Keyshia Cole's song, "Let it Go" serenaded the empty room. Taniesha would've been happy that her favorite song was playing. I ignored the nostalgia and continued down the aisle.

"Paging Wells to the front stage," D.J Trickster called from behind her booth.

My eyes spotted Miss Kimmy near the main stage, and next to her, the thief bitch. Both women laughed loudly at something or someone, reducing my worth to a punchline. Another fit of rage was boiling inside me, ready to erupt. I approached Naima with the urge to punch her smiling face.

"We need to talk."

"That's him?" Miss Kimmy asked with her middle finger up. "You the pastry-dish boy?"

"He's a nobody," she told her and giggled. "Barely legal too. Just a baby boy."

I reached for Naima's arm. She screamed and swung her fists.

"Don't touch her," a deep voice said from behind my back.

I turned around to discover Wells. The buff bouncer stood with his arms crossed.

"Take it easy," Wells said. "No one's going to hurt you. Time to go home, little man."

"No, you don't understand. Naima stole all of my stuff."

"No Naima here, only Siren," he said. "You need to go now."

"She's a thief. Don't you get it? She fucked me."

Wells pointed toward the lobby and then cracked his knuckles.

"Look, I'm trying to be polite," he said with panting breath. "But don't make me throw you out like the last loser. Now go home, boy."

Wells was so focused on my every motion that he was oblivious to both women behind his back, poking out their tongues and crossing their eyes. Anger pushed my steps forward. My hands lifted toward Naima's neck. She backed away with a devilish grin.

"I'm going to kill you," I said.

"You did this," he whispered.

A leg tripped my foot. A boot kicked my stomach. My head collided into darkness.

CHAPTER 11
BOY

*W*ho am I? Where am I going? What am I doing?

Those three questions had been ringing, ringing in my mind all night, perhaps all my life. Near my demise, I hope to have an answer, or at least some clue to the point of it all. Perhaps Socrates was right about seeing an absolute truth after burning from the sunlight, or whatever he and Plato were rambling about in *The Republic*. Long ago, those old farts knew our lives were indeed pointless.

Ring.

If what they said was true, then I would like to die a happy death. Let my last breath give life to butterflies, more beautiful than a pair of big titties. When my body passes away, my spirit will join Keon at eighteen, dead before his prime. My best friend and I will travel through paradise without a destination. Before our departure, I will apologize for not attending his funeral. Through his forgiveness, I will fly free from the burdens of my remorse.

Ring. Ring.

"What is this ringing like sirens?" I asked the cold breeze.

No one was around to listen or save me. The Garden of Eden was dark and lifeless like the rest of San Francisco. I was God's lonely man, abandoned and left to die alone under the dim Market streetlight.

Ring. Ring. Ring.

Unable to ignore the ringing like sirens, I sat upright from the fetal position. A sharp pain screamed from the back of my head. I rubbed behind my scalp, but my hand revealed no blood, only a yellow brownish liquid.

Ring. Ring. Ring. Ring.

The same moist stain was on my pants, on my shoes, and on the sidewalk where I laid. The chunky puddle emitted a fragrance of throw-up, piss, and...*shit*, the head pain grew angrier, spreading throughout my body's midsection. I hugged my stomach tight, as though my organs were getting sodomized.

RING. This pain was for Trevon and Taniesha. *RING.* This punishment was for Hulk-smashing them at the prom. *RING*. These reminders were signs that I was neither favored nor special. God hated me. *RING*.

A scream erupted from my lungs.

A sudden silence. The ringing had stopped, or was it never there?

My body crawled around the puddle of evidence then along the sidewalk until I worked up the strength to lift my legs. *Left. Right. Left. Right.* I needed to play coach in order for my feet to move. A short walk that would have normally taken about thirty seconds had extended past five minutes. Slowly yet surely, I reached the end of Market and Larkin Street, motivated by one intention: Get the hell out of San Francisco.

First, I needed to find the Mercedes and figure out how to start the engine without a key. Maybe I could jimmy the wires like in the movies or find some way to call AAA to start the car. Then I needed to drive as far as possible, just escape to a new life in a better world. My paradise was lost. Perhaps my best friend was the lucky one.

"Keon!"

After finishing my lap around both sides of the street, I discovered my father's car nowhere in sight.

Where did I park the Mercedes?

Not on the next block.

Did the car drive off?

Not across the corner.

Did the car get towed?

Not after the next street.

Did someone jack the car?

Every time I stopped my search and paused, the pain unsettled my insides. With a shake of the head, my body marched up Market Street, zigzagging between the side streets, only to come full circle somehow. My feet had walked so far that nothing looked familiar anymore.

"Why do I give a fuck about the Mercedes?"

My father loved the car more than his oldest son. He could buy another one, maybe two of the same kind if he wanted. Before handing me the car keys, my father had said, "Don't do anything that will dishonor the family." He already had little faith in me making the right decisions. Any glimmer left would likely diminish after discovering my pointless night.

"I hate faith."

Faith was fear spoken through prayer. The waiting in waning days. The belief of a foreseeable relief. Faith was a lie like my father. Let him bear witness to my fall from grace. Let him see my bent knee to the concrete. Let him watch my stretched hands to the sky. Now faith would hear my lonely cries.

"Hey God, it's me again. Fuck you and your pointless tests. I'm sick and tired of feeling sick and tired, but you knew that already. So go ahead. Unleash your wrath. I quit."

"Hey," a deep voice spoke.

"God?" I opened my eyes. Bright lights. "I'm ready."

"You hear me nigga," a man shouted from a taxi window. "Get the fuck out the street."

The taxi stopped several feet from my crouched body. I stood up from the middle of the street and tapped on the yellow hood. A grizzly white head poked out the driver-side window. His gray chiseled face appeared mean and strict like Clint Eastwood with road rage. My arms waved frantically, signaling the man not to drive away.

"Sorry to bother you, sir. Could I get a ride over the bridge, please?"

"Too late to take trips that far, boy," he said and looked at his dashboard clock. "B.A.R.T running right now, or in an hour."

I wiped my sweat with my bandaged hand, and then quickly dropped it to my side.

"I've been out here for a long time. No one can pick me up. I want to go home."

"You try the police?" he asked and laughed. "I don't normally pick up folks like you at this hour. Where are you trying to go?"

"Oakland, sir."

"Figures. Now listen, I don't want no trouble."

"Do I look like someone who will give you trouble?"

"You look like a boy who gave up a long time ago."

The driver mumbled some inaudible words and studied my appearance from head to toe. He scratched his patchy gray hair while the taxi sat parked, engine running. I walked to the passenger window and showed him my closed wallet.

"I have money."

"You should've started with that," he said. "Hurry on up and get in, but don't leave any shit on my seats."

His pale finger pointed to my bandaged hands and stained pants.

"Okay, yes, I promise. You won't regret it. Thank you so much, sir. You saved my life."

"Remember, no trouble," he said with a heavy sigh.

My hand opened the door with quickness. My body jumped in the back, disarming all insecurities. Doubt still lingered in my mind, regret for asking the driver for a ride. My empty wallet could co-sign to the lies. The longer I stayed in the city, the worse my hell grew.

Relief sank in once the taxi drove onto the Bay Bridge toward Oakland and familiarity. My body fell into the backseat like an upright bed. Everything began to dissolve into a soft haze.

Outside my window, a full moon focused on the vehicle. The white orb stared at the back seat. My eyes could no longer stay attentive. My vision grew blurry.

"Stardust never scatters..."

"Get the fuck out the lane, you slow bitch!"

My eyes jolted open. The taxi was tailgating a black Acura.

"Fucking rice rockets," the taxi driver shouted and honked the horn.

The dashboard clock read 4:50 a.m. I had lost track of time ever since I left my phone and watch at the Garden of Eden. Somehow, I had lost the Mercedes at the same time I lost my mind. Where did I go wrong? Why do I feel so broken?

"Is this the end, my only friend, the end?" I sang to myself.

"You woke?" he asked.

The old man grunted, choked up, and spat outside his window. A mist of particles sprayed my face. He peered into the rear-view mirror and inspected the back seat.

"And I tremble lest the darkness teach me that nothing matters," I recited and clapped.

"What's wrong with you?" he asked.

"Ah...I...I had a dream."

"Who's you supposed to be Martin Luther King?" he joked and laughed to himself.

I double checked my flat wallet and then looked out the window.

"We're about to get off the bridge," he said. "You didn't say where you wanted to go."

"I want, just drive me, okay, drop me off by Lake Merritt."

My mind reminisced about Keon, and our three-and-half-mile walks around the lake every other Sunday. My best friend and I would wear thick sunglasses and pretend to act like the Blues Brothers. When we weren't judging the backsides of female joggers, he and I would sit on the bench and gaze at the water and ducks. Keon would describe the Oakland scenery like a Monet painting. He would say everything had meaning and then recite a quote of random literature out of nowhere. Last time we spoke at the lake, Keon had told me, "Never did nature say one thing and wisdom another." He gave me a book of quotations. Written on the inside was the Langston Hughes poem, "Teacher." I wish I could've told him how much he meant to me.

"Could you answer something, boy?" the taxi driver asked. "Did you get back from a formal, or was it like a prom or something?"

"Prom, and my name ain't boy."

"Damn, I knew I was right."

His fingers snapped in excitement. His hand quickly returned to the steering wheel.

"Shouldn't you be at a Denny's hugged up with a little cutie by now?" he asked. "I remember my prom, shit was...hold up...Class of seventy-nine, I think, or one of them years. When you get my age, you forget about school. All I remember was her name, Bethany or Betty, yeah, that's right. I think she was blonde, young, maybe about sixteen. She was begging for a squirting. You ever make a girl squirt?"

I shook my head in fatigue. My eyes searched the back of his scalp for a mute button. He paused and glanced at the rear-view mirror as if sensing my stare. Then his fingers tapped the "two bits" tune onto the steering wheel.

Dah-di-di-dah-di, di-di.

"You could tell when a girl wants it," he said. "Don't try listening to them though. Women folk don't know what they're talking about half the time. They do that, 'No, yes, no, I don't know' bullshit. That's why a man got to tell a woman what she wants, but you probably don't know much about that. Looks like you got pussy whipped. Wait, what was I talking about? Oh yeah, after the prom, me and Betty shacked up in this motel around the Wharf. I laid her down and gave her the old Russian, my favorite. You know about the Russian, right boy?"

When our eyes matched again, my gaze retreated out the window. The taxi connected to the 580 east. I could recognize the Kaiser hospital standing like a monolith near the freeway overpass. The window lights were on along the whole building, calling me toward my safe space.

What if Dr. Imani is in her office?

My therapist could help me. But what else could she do except more recommendations. More group sessions. More creative expression. More appointments with the psychiatrist to prescribe more medication to make me more of a zombie.

"No more."

"Listen boy," he said, oblivious to my whisper. "A Russian is when you slide your dick between a bitch's tits like you're fucking her chest. Don't ask me why it's called a Russian. It sounds better than tit-fucking though. So, when we were at the motel, I remember cumming all on Bethany's tits and neck and face. Oh, oh, oh, that shit was amazing. My first wife wasn't into all that cumshot business. She hated the smell or some bullshit. I see it as you're giving the old man upstairs a 'fuck you' every time you cum anywhere except the pussy. They say the damn earth is going to look like Mars in a thousand years, so fuck it. If the human race is just going to die one day, I say never get a bitch pregnant, but you don't seem to have that problem. By the look of things, you got no, no, no pussy tonight. Couldn't get the dick up or what? I thought you niggas are usually begging for something to cream in. Wait, don't tell me your little bitch ran off with some other nigga fella? I'm just joking, boy. I ain't had no one to clown with all night. How about you and I go around the tracks and pick up some snatch? Now speak up boy."

A laugh spilled from his lips. My arm lifted into the air. My fist collided into his scalp. His forehead smacked into the steering wheel. I bounced back into the seat. The taxi drifted into the emergency lane. The car shifted to park. The headlights shut off. He removed his seat belt.

"Give me the money you owe and get the fuck out," he commanded and rubbed his head.

"I don't have any money."

My eyes searched outside for help, finding no cars or lights on the freeway, only a black mass from afar. The darkness revealed no allies. God made me his lonely man in the face of hell.

"Okay, you don't have any money," he mumbled.

His body leaned toward the passenger seat. His hand reached into the glove compartment.

"Okay, let's see if you don't have money."

The taxi driver repeated the same words over and over again as his hands rummaged through the compartment clutter. He pulled out a dirty screwdriver and pushed his door open. His feet stomped out the car. His hands opened my door and pulled me out by my shirt collar. His teeth clenched as he lunged at my side with the screwdriver, nearly piercing my ribs.

"You owe me *sixty-eight fifty,* boy!" he shouted and growled. His hot breath pressed on my face. "Give it to me, or I'll make you wish you had enough."

"I don't have anything. Can we just work something out?"

"See I told you, I ain't want no trouble," he said. "No, you did this."

He raised the screwdriver's dull tip to my right eye. I pulled my pockets inside-out.

"Please sir, don't kill me. I'm sorry, please don't kill me, please."

He lowered the screwdriver and began to shake my body back and forth, expecting some kind of change to fall out from my pants. The sudden jerking caused an adverse effect.

"Oh my God!"

Without warning, my mouth vomited whatever was left in my stomach onto the sidewalk. The man jumped back as though my puke was poisonous.

"No, I didn't mean to ask for a ride. I don't want to die. No, I just want my mama."

My eyes bursted in tears. I used my shirt sleeve to wipe my wet mouth and runny nose.

"Mama!"

"Quit your crying boy," the taxi driver shouted. "Nobody cares."

He tucked the screwdriver into his pocket and retraced his steps to the car.

"Stupid fucking niggas. Never again, never *again*."

The grumpy man repeated his curses over and over until his old body was back inside the taxi. He slammed the door and drove off into the dark freeway.

"Nobody knows the troubles I've seen, nobody knows but Jesus..."

Left stranded, shocked, and defeated, my dry lips took it upon themselves to sing, "Nobody knows the troubles I've seen," a song my mama would often harmonize at home. When I was younger, she had taught me the lyrics as a way to bring calm to my storms. With nothing else to do, my lips sang the church melody and marched as if I was going to my own funeral.

"Nobody knows the trouble I've seen, glory hallelujah..."

My body walked along the emergency lane for fifteen, maybe twenty minutes. My eyes were halfway open for most of the journey. My mind blanked out into a foggy daze. The only part that felt real was the loneliness keeping me company from beginning to end.

I thought about my mama's compassion. My father's strength. My little brother's joy. Trevon's friendship. Taniesha's affection. Raymond's wisdom. The cigarette lady's advice. Pater's solitude. Wice's savagery. Wells' assertiveness. The stripper's attention. The taxi driver's generosity. I remembered Keon, the big brother I never had, and what he would've done if put in my position.

My heart wanted to apologize to everyone. Somehow, they tried to help me, hoping I would change, but their faith just didn't work out. Not because of their efforts, time, or God. My failure was no one's fault but my own.

"Now I know why there's no cure to the common birthday."

My eyes had been crying for a long time. My mind had stopped noticing at some point on the freeway. Eventually, I found an off-ramp and marched downhill.

When I arrived on Broadway Street, my body continued walking toward the Kaiser building, my safe space where Dr. Imani helped me after Keon's death. My feet stopped at the first bench in sight, somewhere in Mosswood Park. My hands glided along the yellow sign.

"Looking for a better home?"

A Black boy stood across the street, staring my way. He wore a tuxedo like mine. His face resembled my little brother's. The boy smiled like he smiled that evening, or the day before, or whatever time it was when his silence refused to let me go. No, I couldn't leave Steven like Keon left me. If not to live for myself, I must live for others, or what's the point to it all?

A sudden dawn approached from afar. The night's shadow had dissolved. Streetlamps awoke before the sun. In the spotlight was a beige Mercedes double-parked on the curb.

The boy had disappeared.

He was never there.

EPILOGUE
PINOCCHIO

S aturday 9:11 a.m.

"I guess that's everything, Judge Tarver," Officer Williams said and exhaled.

He studied my father for confirmation. They traded glances and nodded, signaling to an understanding I might have misunderstood.

"I'm going to check on the Mercedes again, sir."

"Update me on the report when it arrives, please," my father said and crossed his arms. He leaned against the opposite wall of the jail cell. "Thank you for finding my boy...my son."

"I'll come back in a couple minutes," Officer Williams said and left us alone.

The gate closed.

My holding cell was crowded with the silence of two people. The only items left in the small gray cage were a narrow cot bolted to the ground, a dark air vent, and a plastic chair and kid's desk with crayons, a yellow notepad, and a worn copy of the book, Pinocchio.

Outside were rustling breaths and scattered steps. A deep laugh echoed down the corridor. Claps rang throughout the hallway. In the next cell, an inmate shouted curses in between pleads for freedom.

"Let me out, let me out!" the man shouted.

My bruised hands covered my ears from the rage. Within my earmuff silence, I could hear my lungs panting for relief. My heart drummed like a trap beat. My body was still running on adrenaline, yet my soul yearned for sleep. My heavy head fell back onto the hard cot. My tired eyes gazed at the white ceiling with dark spots. My exhausted mind began to doze off from all of the deep reflection. After confessing to my whole twelve-hour story, there was nothing left to say or do, but breathe.

"Can I take a nap?" I asked and yawned.

"I can't believe you'd ask that," my father said.

He glanced outside the cell and checked to see if anyone was nearby.

"Hell no. You're lucky your mother ain't here. Both of us would've whooped your ass."

"I don't care if she's with Steven. I just wish she was here instead of you."

His leg kicked the cot. Startled, my body sat up and acted as if I was paying attention.

"Listen, there are a few things I still don't understand. You parked the Mercedes in San Francisco, right? And when you returned from the brothel, or strip club or whatever, the car wasn't there, right? So, then you took a taxi, and the driver assaulted you because you punched him and had no money, but wait, you had no money because some stripper with a fake name stole everything, right? And then the officer found you on a park bench at the same hospital where you go for therapy. Nah, this can't be right. I mean, this is all a bit too hard to chew. Is there anything else you may have missed or imagined?"

"I don't know."

My body leaned back onto the cot. Something poked my butt cheek. My hand slid into my back pocket and pulled out the purple neon bracelet with Taneisha's name.

"I guess, I won't be needing this anymore. Can you give it to her, please?"

"It's best to keep every hope you have."

His finger twirled like a conductor, directing me to put the bracelet back into my pocket.

"Listen, how long were you sleeping at the park? The officer told me privately about a report. A young Black male at Mosswood after midnight. I don't want to, but I have to ask."

"No," I whispered and yawned again. "I don't know."

My father also yawned, but his hand quickly covered his mouth.

"I told you before that's contagious," he said.

"What's contagious?" I asked and rested my eyes.

"That same song: 'I don't know, I don't know,' you love to sing."

His leg kicked the cot again, jolting my body to sit up.

"You and your mother are both like broken records," he said and raised his voice. "And you haven't said a thing about your hands. They're the ones that really look broken."

"Fine, I'm fine. I'm just tired."

"You're tired? Listen, I'm tired of not knowing how my car got to Mosswood Park. Now sit up straight and talk with your mouth."

My body refused to move to his commands, so my lips spoke instead.

"Why does the car even matter? Why does anything matter at this point? Just be honest, do you still love me?"

"Come on Jonah, what kind of question is that? I love you, but I don't think you love yourself. Why would a boy with every privilege in the world want to escape from his life and run away? Is it because you think I'm a horrible father? I really don't understand. Maybe, if I had been there more for you and your brother in the beginning, maybe..."

"We'll never know."

My father shook his head in disbelief. He continued pacing around the cell in circles, mumbling to himself, and rattling his head nervously. He moved to the desk, sat in the chair, and breathed deeply. He pretended to take interest in the Pinocchio book, flipping through the pages as casual as he was dressed. To my surprise, I had never seen this vulnerable side of him before.

On weekdays, my father usually wore a suit and tie to work. On weekends, he often wore a Polo sweater and Birkenstock sandals at home. But on this special Saturday morning, my father neglected to dress formally at his place of work. He sported his Los Angeles Rams snapback and a gray Star Trek shirt with Spock's long ears stretched on the front. His feet rocked his old Iverson Reebok shoes, which he only wore when tending the lawn or backyard. His bushy eyes were covered by his black aviator glasses to mask his fatigue. His weary face was in deep concentration like I had been when sharing my twelve-hour journey.

Maybe my father was rehearsing the story he would tell my mama and little brother. Perhaps he was imagining the act he would put on to his colleagues during work tomorrow. But no one would talk bad about Judge Tarver's disgraceful son. He wasn't in this cell for me. My father was here to save his reputation.

"Tell me the truth," I asked. "What's going to happen to Taniesha and Trevon?"

"Your friends," he said with a sigh and closed the Pinocchio book. "They're in the hospital. Taniesha might be fine after a few days. Trevon, well, he's receiving the best care, but I don't know. He's roughed up pretty bad. We'll be lucky if they don't press charges, on account if anyone can get their stories straight. *Jesus,* I don't understand. What came over you? Was it your meds? We know you stopped taking them, but did one of your friends slip you something? We know about the mixed drinks at prom; however, I know there's more you haven't told me."

"That's all I remembered."

"You don't understand Jonah, you committed an assault and battery."

His hand smacked the desk. My body flinched in defense.

"If they press charges, the court can try you as an adult. If convicted, they'll send your ass up to Santa Rita. You'll be another criminal, another Black thug, just another *nigga*. Damnit, why didn't you think before, no, it'll be okay. We'll be okay. I know we will."

"I'm scared of the future. What will happen to me?"

"You'll be okay, Jonah, you'll be okay," he repeated, each time with more uncertainty.

His body shivered. His words mumbled. His glossy eyes stared at the book cover.

"Let me think. If it comes down to it, you'll have the best team set up for your defense. Maybe we'll make a plea of temporary insanity, on account of your bi, I mean, your mental capacity. I'm sorry, but for now, you're in jail until the bond comes through. I still can't believe it. Out of all the places in the world, you're here for your birthday. There's still no cure for..."

"Noooo," I shouted and stretched out my hands. "Please don't."

"What did I say?" he asked with his brows raised.

"No, no, it's just that this place ain't so bad," I lied and forced a smile. "There's a book."

My father picked up the soft bound text and moved beside me on the cot. His long arms wrapped around my back and pulled me close to his warm body. At first, I flinched, somewhat unfamiliar to his affection. My eyes shifted to the book in his hand: *The Adventures of Pinocchio by Carlos Collodi.* An illustration of a smiling wooden boy stood on the front cover.

"Do you remember when I used to read this to you?" he asked and opened the book.

"I never really understood it. The movie version was better, even though they made the Geppetto dude look like a pedo. Hey look, there's a bunch of annotations in here. This one says: *'Woe to those boys who rebel against their parents and run away capriciously from home. They will never come to any good in the world and sooner or later they will repent bitterly.'* Why highlight that part? Wait, did you plant this here or something?"

"This was your favorite book when you were younger, when you were in your Lego phase," he said with a proud smile and rubbed my back. "You'd act out the characters and voices like a puppeteer. Now your brother acts the same way with his toys, and he's reading all the time like you. There's so much imagination between the two of you."

"I wonder why."

"I know Keon played a big role in that, especially since he was able to support you in ways I couldn't. I miss that young man. He was like a big brother to you. He was like my third son, so I feel his loss too. You're not alone in pain."

My father paused. His eyes clenched tight, wet at the sides.

"There's something you need to know. As the oldest, I expect you to become the man of the house when I'm not around."

I crossed my arms and shook my head.

"I already know what you're about to say. You and mama are getting a divorce. I figured it out a while ago."

My father's smile quickly dropped to a frown.

"I knew you were too smart for your own good, but no, that's not it. Yes, your mother threatened divorce, but she stopped bugging me about alimony after she found the doctor's report in my office."

"What doctor's report?"

"Listen son, you know how I would drop you off at your therapy sessions and pick you up afterwards? What you didn't know was that I had my own appointments scheduled at the same time. I had neglected seeing a doctor for so long out of shame and fear. I guess, you can call it Black man's pride. I didn't want anyone to know and worry, but now it's getting worse."

"What's worse? What are you talking about?"

"I need you to listen."

My father held onto my hand with a tense grip. His wrists were trembling.

"Dad."

"Son, I have prostate cancer, stage three."

"*Prostate cancer*? No, no I don't believe you. You can't have cancer. You're my dad."

"I've been hiding it for over a year."

"No. How could you hide cancer? This can't be true. Why tell me now?"

"Because most people will deny hard truths instead of face them."

I gripped his hand tighter than I ever had in my life. My dad took several deep breaths, and I quickly followed his lead. His hands lifted mine onto my chest. My heart was beating as fast as my tears were falling.

"Relax, be still," he said and pulled out a folded tissue paper. "Don't you see? You manned up before I did. You asked for help and got the best care Kaiser could offer. You inspired me to do the same, but it might be too late."

My lips trembled. My nose sniffled. My body quivered as if crippled by the truth.

"No, it can't be too late. This isn't really happening. No, tell me you'll be okay."

Slowly, his warm hand wiped my wet face and nose and then handed me the tissue.

"Be still, and just relax, son."

"*Relax?* How can I relax?" I shouted and threw the tissue on the ground. "Now I know there's no point to anything when we're just a bunch of broken pencils."

"No, you've said that several times before, but I see it differently. You can have a broken pencil and still be able to write. A dull point can still illustrate a meaningful story. Just because Keon's life was cut short doesn't mean he didn't leave a memorable story behind. His life was one worth reading like mine, and yours, and the countless lives before and after ours. We might feel broken, but we are what remains from damage. Son, do you understand what I'm saying?"

"Yes, but, but, but I can't lose nobody else. No, you're the only dad I have. I need you."

His arms pulled me close and held me tight. I couldn't remember the last time we hugged.

"We will find happiness, my heart. You are my pride and joy, so I will always love you. No matter what. Everything I did for you and this family was to make sure everyone was happy. That's all I ever wanted. Are you happy, son? Nothing else matters."

Tap. Tap. Tap.

"Excuse me Judge Tarver," Officer Williams interrupted. "We need to talk."

He tapped once more on the gate door. In his hand held a plastic bag with my phone, watch, and car keys. Within moments, he will share the news I already knew.

"It's urgent," he said with a frown and nod.

My dad kissed my forehead and whispered a prayer that I could barely hear, except for the last words: *"And lead us not into temptation but deliver us from evil."*

"Amen," we both said in harmony.

He looked me in my eyes and asked, "Son, do you know how to be happy?"

I sat silent within my dad's embrace. He released his hug and then followed Officer Williams out of the cell. In the hallway, they spoke into one another's ear. Both heads shook with disappointment. My dad fell into Williams' open arms, and then blurted, "It's all my fault!"

My body sat up straight on the hard cot. My hand opened the Pinocchio book to another highlighted passage. My eyes read the words. My mind drifted off into a different world again.

If I remain, I shall'nt escape the fate of all other boys. I shall be sent to school and shall be made to study either by love or by force. To tell you in confidence, I have no wish to learn. It is much more amusing to run after butterflies, or to climb trees and to take the young birds out of their nests.

"I know."

BROKEN
PENCILS

J.R. RICE

TO Be CONTINUED...

About The Author

J.R. Rice is a Black man, writer, teacher, and spoken word artist, born and raised in Oakland, California. He has a B.A in Creative Writing and an English Education teaching credential from California State University of Long Beach. While studying abroad in Greece, he was mentored by the author, George Crane. His novella, Broken Pencils earned the 2024 Literary Titan Gold Book Award, the Literary Global Gold Award, Third place in Best African-American Literature and Best New Fiction in the 2024 Firebird Book Award contest, and has made the 2024 Hawthorne Prize Shortlist. He now resides and teaches in the Bay Area, California. To learn more about J.R. Rice, please visit his website at www.jrrice.com.

Printed in the USA
CPSIA information can be obtained
at www.ICGtesting.com
JSHW041902160624
64868JS00015B/128